IT WAS AN ODD TIME
FOR A PRESS CONFERENCE.

The basketball season was just three games old, so it was too early for a coaching change. There were no unsigned draft choices, no major trades in the offing. In fact, the Lakers were among the most stable and successful franchises in all of sports. What it took, however, was simply a single word to turn this press conference into the potential source of a major story. And that word was . . .

. . . *Magic!*

MAGIC

MORE THAN A LEGEND

A BIOGRAPHY
by Bill Gutman

HarperPaperbacks
A Division of HarperCollins*Publishers*

HarperPaperbacks *A Division of* HarperCollins*Publishers*
10 East 53rd Street, New York, N.Y. 10022

Cover photographs by John McDonough/Sports Illustrated

First printing: January 1992

Printed in the United States of America

HarperPaperbacks and colophon are trademarks of HarperCollins*Publishers*

❖ 10 9 8 7 6 5 4 3 2 1

CONTENTS

──PROLOGUE──

A PRESS CONFERENCE IN THE SPORTS world usually means rounding up the usual suspects. The local newspapers, wire services, TV and radio stations go through the obligatory motions and send their reporters to the gathering. But when the Los Angeles Lakers called the press together at the Great Western Forum in Inglewood on the afternoon of November 7, 1991, there was a hint of something decidedly more than routine in the air. And as the 3:00 P.M., Pacific Coast starting time approached, the rumors began swirling around in a growing crescendo of speculation.

It was an odd time for a press conference. The basketball season was just three games old, so it was too early for a coaching change. There were no unsigned draft choices, no major trades in the offing. In fact, the Lakers were among the most stable and successful franchises in all of sports. What it took, however, was simply a single word to turn this press conference into the potential source of a major story. And that word was . . .

. . . *Magic!*

When used as a proper noun in the context of the sports world, *Magic* immediately conjures up an image of talent, style, and grace. These are only some of the qualities of Earvin "Magic" Johnson, the mercurial superstar of the Los Angeles Lakers, the man who brought *showtime* to the Great Western Forum while leading his team to five world championships and carving out a career that had already become legendary.

But why should an early-season press conference involve Magic Johnson? Most of the media was puzzled. The only trace of a clue was Magic's absence from the first three Laker games of the 1991–92 campaign. Flu-like symptoms and fatigue were the reasons given for his trio of no-shows. Maybe it was something else? An injury, an illness? The guessing game continued until the dais began filling up.

Laker owner Jerry Buss was there. So was Kareem Abdul-Jabbar, the retired Laker center who teamed with Magic on four of the five L.A. title teams. NBA Commissioner David Stern was also present, as was Laker general manager Jerry West. Everyone knew them immediately. But there was still another man sitting quietly near the podium. Only some of the media people knew him. They quickly passed the word. He was Laker team physician Dr. Michael Mellman.

If one didn't know better, it almost looked like some kind of Friar's roast with Magic Johnson the guest of honor, the roastee who would be the target of everyone's jokes and jibes. But the grim expressions on the faces bespoke otherwise. An ominous feeling began to spread slowly among the normally gregarious and wise-cracking reporters. Yet when Magic himself finally stepped in front of the bevy of microphones, not a single person in the large room was prepared for what he was about to say. His announcement would numb even the most grizzled veterans among the newsmen in the room. It was chilling, shocking, and totally unexpected.

Looking poised and collected, occasionally flashing the world-famous smile that had endeared him to so many people, Magic told the group without hesitation that he was retiring from basketball, effective immediately, because he had tested positive for the HIV virus.

At first his words didn't seem to register. It was as if some kind of built-in mechanism deep within the human soul suddenly switched to *reject*. It didn't want to accept the words or process them. It wanted, instead, to carve them up and spit them out. It wanted to program in their place a loud shout of No! Not Magic. Not Magic Johnson.

The HIV virus, a precursor of AIDS, Acquired Immune Deficiency Syndrome. It was a no-win equation, leading to one of the most insidious diseases of the late 20th century. And here was one of the greatest athletes of all time, a man who less than a year and a half earlier had been the Most Valuable Player in the National Basketball Association, telling the world that he had the HIV virus. Within seconds, Magic spoke again.

"I just want to make it clear first of all that I do not have the AIDS disease. I plan on being here for a long time. . . . Life is going to go on for me and I'm going to be a happy man. . . . But sometimes you're a little naive and think 'it's not going to happen to me. It only happens to other people.' But here I am saying that it can happen to anybody. Even me, Magic Johnson."

From there, the press conference took on an almost surrealistic quality. Magic spoke calmly, his voice strong and steady. He looked reporters straight in the eye. He flashed his charismatic smile, the same smile people had been used to seeing ever since he led his Michigan State team to the NCAA championship back in 1979. His commanding presence continued to make his words difficult to believe.

"I'm going to beat it," he said. "Life is going to go on for me and I'm going to be a happy man. I guess now I'll get to enjoy some of the other sides of living. I will still be here enjoying Laker games. Basketball will still be a part of my life. I plan on going on with the Lakers and the league, and I plan on bugging you guys as I always have."

There was nervous laughter in the audience. Minutes later, Magic turned the conference over to Dr. Mellman, who immediately reiterated that his patient did not have the AIDS disease. Magic was still completely healthy. He had been advised, however, to retire from the game he loved because it was felt that the stress of an 82-game basketball season could accelerate the weakening of his immune system. Magic would begin to follow a prescribed program of medication which, hopefully, would forestall the onset of the actual disease. HIV-positive patients, Dr. Mellman said, can sometimes go 10 years or more without showing signs of full-blown AIDS.

Before the conference adjourned, Magic assured reporters that Cookie, his wife of two months, had been tested for the HIV virus and was negative. He also said he planned to become a spokeman in the battle against AIDS and would begin a public-awareness campaign to urge everyone, especially the young, to always practice safe sex.

Then he was gone. The press conference was over

and it was reality time. Broadcasters rushed to get the story on the air. Reporters hit the phones to call their offices. Within minutes, the media blitz was underway. Programs were interrupted all over the country. Magic Johnson was again front page news, as he had been so often during his extraordinary basketball career. Only this time the story transcended sports. It was the story of a very courageous man and it touched the hearts of people from all walks of life and in every corner of the land.

Never before, in fact, had the plight of an athlete affected so many people. But Magic Johnson was more than an athlete. He was a celebrity, an entertainer. Even those who didn't follow his exploits on the basketball court knew him as a spokeman for a myriad of products, or as a talkative, smiling, and articulate guest on a variety of television and radio talk shows. In a media-conscious world where h-y-p-e sometimes carries the connotation of other kinds of four-letter words, Magic was everywhere. Yet there was no feeling of overexposure, no resentment that this 6'9" basketball star was becoming one of the wealthiest men in America. The overwhelming power of his personality wouldn't allow that.

Now he had told the world he had the HIV virus. Unless a cure is found sometime during the next decade, Magic Johnson will eventually become ill with AIDS. One newspaper came right out and said his announcement was tantamount to a death sentence. Yet AIDS was a disease many Americans still preferred to sweep under the rug. They read the stories and heard the statistics but still turned their heads and looked the other way. Like Magic, they felt it couldn't happen to them.

The sports world has always been filled with its own statistics. For basketball aficionados there are points, rebounds, assists, blocks, steals, percentages, triple doubles, etc. You name it. Stats are often the measure of a team and its individuals. Some fans know basketball statistics better than those associated with their own jobs. Heck, the average fan can often tell you Michael Jordan's scoring average quicker than his own wife's age.

But as far as the statistics involving AIDS, well, that's something else. Once Magic made his announcement, however, the numbers began jumping off the pages of newspapers and out of TV screens with sobering regularity. According to the Centers for Disease Control, more than 195,000 Americans have been diagnosed with AIDS since 1981. Of that number, some 126,000 have died. However, the estimate of the number of Americans who might already be HIV-positive and still don't know it runs into the millions. Unlike sports stats, these numbers are frightening . . . and should be.

There had already been a good number of deaths due to AIDS in the entertainment world, most notably, perhaps, the actor Rock Hudson. There had also been several deaths in the sports field, but mostly peripheral or relatively unknown figures—a former NFL player, a fighter, a decathlete, a stock car driver, and a former big league baseball player. But as one writer put it, Magic was the guy who finally brought AIDS into everyone's living room.

"By making his announcement as he did, Magic has saved thousands, maybe even millions of lives," said Gerald Lenoir, executive director of the San Francisco Black Coalition on AIDS.

Many agreed. If Magic Johnson could stand before the world and announce that he was HIV-positive, he would bring a newfound and universal awareness of the disease. In many ways, Magic was larger than life. He was someone people cared about, someone many idolized. He was the guy, along with Michael Jordan, that kids playing hoops on the playgrounds of America most wanted to emulate. Now he was telling them not to make the same mistake he did.

A little more than twenty-four hours after making his startling announcement, Magic was back on national television. This time it was on the *Arsenio Hall Show*. Arsenio was a personal friend, so Magic chose his show as a forum to begin the next phase of his life, bringing AIDS awareness to the same millions of people he had entertained as a basketball star for a dozen wonderful years.

After receiving a compelling standing ovation that lasted some five full minutes, Magic again talked openly about the AIDS virus and what it had done to his life. As always, the smile was there, along with the charisma and commanding presence that had punctuated his athletic career. He told the audience that he had contracted the disease through heterosexual contact, dispelling a widely held notion that only homosexuals and intravenous drug users can contract the virus.

He said again that Cookie, his wife, did not have the virus and that he would go on with his life, still hoping to fulfill his dream of someday being the owner of a professional basketball team. He also said he would continue to be outspoken about the virus and the disease, and would welcome an opportunity to serve on President Bush's National Commission on AIDS, something that would become a reality a short time later. And he urged once more that everyone practice safe sex and be sure to use a condom. It was something most people had been reluctant to say publicly. Magic Johnson didn't hesitate.

The fallout from Magic's announcement began

almost immediately. His friend and greatest rival on the basketball court, Larry Bird of the Boston Celtics, wept when he heard the news and was unable to make a public statement for several days.

"It doesn't seem fair," Bird finally said. "It doesn't seem right. I've been lost for words. . . . All you can do is pray."

Charles Barkley, another NBA superstar known for his toughness and determination on the court, also found words hard to come by.

"I'm just sitting here looking at [Magic's] jersey," Barkley said. "I'm just kind of shaking a little bit. It's really frightening."

Wayne Gretzky, hockey's reigning superstar, admitted that the upper echelon of athletes sometimes feel they are invincible because so many people put them on a pedestal.

"But we bleed, sweat, cry, and have ups and downs like everyone else," Gretzky said. "This was a real jolt."

Pat Riley, who had coached Magic for nearly a decade at Los Angeles and who was currently coaching the New York Knicks, called the announcement "tragic, just tragic." The night after the press conference, Riley led a prayer for Magic right on the court at Madison Square Garden, the players from both the Knicks and their opponents gathered around him.

President Bush called Magic "a hero," adding, "I just can't tell you the high regard I have for this athlete." And the mayor of Los Angeles, Tom Bradley, equated Magic's announcement with a historial tragedy of epic proportions.

Said Bradley, "It was like someone hit me in the stomach with a 300-pound hammer. I can only relate this to one other incident in my memory, and that was the news of President John F. Kennedy being assassinated."

A little farfetched? Maybe, but that's the impact

Earvin Johnson has had on so many people, from the President of the United States and the Mayor of Los Angeles right down to kids in elementary school. Everyone knew Magic and felt he was their friend.

He had come into our lives with a smile on his face, leading his school to a national championship in prime time right before our eyes. When he entered the National Basketball Association he brought his boyish exuberance with him, as well as a special passion for the art of the game and a wealth of physical talent. Along with Larry Bird, Magic is given credit for rescuing a sport that was having financial and image difficulties, and helping to turn it into a multi-million dollar business.

In addition, he is also given credit for revolutionizing the game. He was a 6'9" point guard, the guy who handled the basketball, directed traffic on the court, and made the Laker offense go. That put him in a position that had been once the exclusive domain of the "small" man. But he showed immediately that he could do all the things with a basketball that smaller and quicker players could do. And he used every one of his skills to the utmost advantage.

He was also one of the rare athletes with the ability to make those around him better players. It was the strength of his will and his leadership ability that enabled his teammates to raise the level of their games. In other words, he was a winner. There were, of course, many rewards for his talents. His team won five world championships during the 1980s. A perennial all-star, he was also the league's Most Valuable Player three times and the MVP of the playoffs on three occasions.

That wasn't all. Magic was the guy who invented the term the "triple double." That's because of the number of times he hit double figures in scoring, rebounding, and assists all in the same game. It was almost routine with him. In addition, he became the NBA's all-time assist leader in his final season, surpassing the record set by another basketball legend, Oscar Robertson. To Magic, this was the ultimate achievement because it showed the kind of team player he was. Otherwise, individual statistics meant little to him. It was winning that meant everything.

"A player like Magic comes along once every 20 years," said Lakers general manager Jerry West, himself a former all-time great. "You have no idea of how difficult it is to be great every night, year after year. It's a stressful situation, but Magic pulled it off. And in doing so, he gave his teammates courage."

Off the court, Magic was determined to dispel the notion of the "dumb jock." During his career he also became known as one of the sport world's best and smartest businessmen. His endorsement income far outstripped his more-than-generous NBA salary, and his outside investments and business interests made him an extremely wealthy man. His ambition to become the first black athlete to eventually own a basketball team would, in his eyes, make the transition complete.

Yet unlike many so-called superstars, Magic never "copped" an attitude. He never gave an inch less than his best on the court and never ceased to be courteous and generous off the court. Much of his time and energy was devoted to charitable work. His efforts on behalf of the United Negro College Fund have netted some $6 million over the years.

But there are also other examples, some seemingly insignificant, from which to get an accurate measure of the man. For example, there was the time a local high school player approached him and asked him to buy candy to help finance uniforms for the team. Magic promptly bought the uniforms for the entire team. Even in the summer of 1991, before he learned the news that would end his career, he was still all about giving. Abe Pollin, the owner of the Washington Bullets, was having trouble finding celebrities to attend a fund-raiser he was chairing. When he heard about it, Magic not only volunteered to be there, but took over the entire event and helped raise some $200,000. These are things he didn't have to do. But just try to stop him.

For these reasons, Magic Johnson had become a larger-than-life figure when he told the world he was HIV-positive. The only previous situation in sports that could be remotely equated to Magic's stunning announcement happened back in 1939. That was when Lou Gehrig, the famed "Iron Horse" of the New York Yankees, learned he had a fatal disease and only a short time to live. Gehrig said his farewell before a tear-stained, packed house at Yankee Stadium in New York.

While the outpouring of emotion for Gehrig was great, it was confined mainly to the New York area. There was no national television back then, no widespread media explosion that would carry Gehrig's plight to every nook and corner of the country. Gehrig was already ill and a dying man at the time. Everyone knew it. While Magic may ultimately suffer the same fate, his announcement was almost a celebration of life. That's how upbeat and positive he remained through it all.

Gehrig, of course, is rememembered for the now-famous concluding words of his farewell speech when he said, "Today, I consider myself the luckiest man on the face of the earth."

For Magic Johnson, the message was similar. When first told about the virus his first reaction was, "I'll deal with it." He also told people that he had no fear of death. "If I die tomorrow, next year or whenever it might be, I'll know I've had a great life."

CHAPTER ONE

The Early Years

HOW DOES A YOUNGSTER FROM A FAMI-
ly of ten children become one of
the finest athletes and most recog-
nizable men in America? It isn't simply because he has
natural physical gifts. That helps. But to make it to the
top takes a special kind of person with both the innate
and the acquired qualities necessary to persevere. It
also takes a combination of hard work and sacrifice,
and those were traits young Earvin Johnson learned
early just from watching his parents.

Once, when his former coach Pat Riley was talking
about Magic's ability to distribute the basketball from
all angles on the court, he jokingly said that Magic was
born passing. It's a cute image, but passing a basketball
was the last thing Christine and Earvin Johnson, Sr.,

were thinking about on August 14, 1959, when the fourth of their seven children was born. Mr. Johnson also had three children he brought with him when he married Magic's mother. Maybe he had some kind of premonition, because it was the son born in 1959 upon whom he bestowed his name.

The Johnsons lived in Lansing, Michigan, a mid-sized city dominated by the automobile and construction industries. Their small, yellow frame house on Middle Street where Magic grew up was in the heart of the city, in what Magic himself called a lower middle-class area. Lansing was not nearly the size of Detroit, for example, so a lot of the problems that exist in big-city ghetto areas could be avoided in Lansing. If they were there, it was on a much smaller scale.

Magic did not, however, grow up in a ghetto. He described the neighborhood as mostly black, the people religious, hardworking, and clean-living. Many came to Lansing during the 1950s and '60s when the automobile industry was thriving and had a much greater need for help than it does today.

Earvin, Sr., was one of many who came up from the south in search of work. He was born in Wesson, Mississippi, where, like many rural blacks, he was raised on a farm. It was a sharecropper situation where the tenants were supposed to get half of what they produced. But, unfortunately, that wasn't always the case.

Mr. Johnson's mother brought him to Chicago in 1942 when he was just seven, but later sent him back to Mississippi to live with his grandparents. He was back and forth several more times before leaving home for good at nineteen and heading north once more. His search for a good job eventually brought him to Lansing and the Fisher Body Corporation. After a year with Fisher Body, Mr. Johnson was drafted into the service.

While in the army he met and ultimately married Magic's mother.

She, too, was from the south, having been raised in North Carolina. Magic remembers hearing stories from her about the pristine beauty of the rural south and said she always felt bad that none of her children had the opportunity to experience life there.

After his time in the service was up, the Johnsons returned to Lansing. Mr. Johnson got his job back at Fisher Body and the two began adding to their family. It was then that Magic's father began a routine he would continue for nineteen years, that of juggling two full-time jobs in order to support his family.

He began working on an assembly line that produced Oldsmobile bodies. His job was operating a grinding boot, a machine that smoothed out metal and could be dangerous. He would often come home with burns in his clothing and sometimes on his skin. After a while, he was promoted to intermediate relief man, a job he would continue to hold for years. His second job at first was pumping gas. Eventually, he was able to borrow the money to buy an old truck and used it to start his own business cleaning up stores and shops, as well as hauling trash.

It was a demanding schedule. Magic remembers him working at Fisher Body from four in the afternoon until one in the morning. He would then clean some of the shops on his route for a couple of hours, then come home to catch a few hours sleep. By 9:00 A.M. he was back collecting the trash that had to go to the dump. After that was done, he would have maybe two or three hours to rest before it was back to Fisher Body and the beginning of another shift.

Despite his hard work and perseverence, the money still wasn't always enough, and once Magic's twin sisters were old enough, his mother took a full-time job as a school custodian. She did that in addition to cleaning house, cooking, and taking care of her large family. Magic recalls seeing both his parents exhausted from their daily grind, and as a youngster he promised his mother that he was going to make something out of himself so that she would never have to work again. It's apparent, however, that the work ethic shown by both his parents made an impression on young Earvin. It gave him not only a motivation to succeed, but also a means by which to do it. Nothing, he learned early on, came easy.

The kids in the neighborhood didn't have a whole lot, but they spent a great deal of time on the streets, playing all kinds of games and eventually sports. At home, the Johnson children got along well. Their mother was usually the disciplinarian simply because their father was gone so much. She was the arbitrator of the normal squabbles and arguments between the kids and always emphasized closeness and love. Mr. and Mrs. Johnson were both religious people, attending church every week. All their children were actively involved in church activities, serving as ushers and members of the choir.

Fortunately, none of the Johnson children was ever in major trouble with the law. While Mrs. Johnson handled the minor disciplinary problems, she always had a trump card. If things seemed to be getting out of hand, she threatened to inform the "Big E," the nickname given Magic's father. The kids all knew how hard he worked and how tired he was when he finally came home. As a consequence, none of them wanted to make him mad.

Magic does admit to one transgression at the age of nine. He and his friends decided to test their bravery by stealing some candy and balloons from a neighborhood store. Not surprisingly, they were caught and that was

one time the Big E was called in. A couple of hard licks
with a strap cured Magic once and for all. He was also
ashamed that he had let his parents down. His father
admonished him for stealing, adding that if he ever
wanted anything, he should ask for it. If it couldn't be
had, the Big E said, then he would have to do without.

By the time he was in the third grade at the Main
Street elementary school, young Earvin was beginning
to play basketball, the game that would eventually
become his passion and his life. Aside from his family,
it was truly his first love. It was at the Main Street
school that he first met another third-grader named Jay
Vincent. Jay went to the Holmes Street School. The two
boys would remain friendly rivals right through high
school, then would be united as teammates at Michigan
State.

Basketball wasn't much more than a kind of helter-
skelter activity in those early years. The boys were just
learning the game and often didn't even adhere to the
rules. But it was fun. The eight-foot high hoops enabled
the youngsters to shoot without too much strain. But at
that time, a casual observer would not have spotted any
future Oscar Robertsons, Elgin Baylors, or Bill Russells
out there.

Young Earvin kept playing, however, and pretty
soon learned he had a talent for the game. He also had
to learn about priorities. When his fifth-grade team was
about to play the Michigan Avenue School in a championship game, he learn he had been grounded by a
teacher for not turning in an assignment. No matter
how hard he protested, she wouldn't let him play. His
mother upheld the sentence, which for a fifth-grader
must have seemed excessive to the point that he felt
his life was ruined.

Before long, Earvin was like a lot of other young
boys who discover they can assert themselves through

sports. He began to live and breathe for the game. It was his identification, his earliest passion. What that meant was driving his mother crazy by bouncing a basketball wherever he went, usually in the house. And when Christine Johnson took the ball away, young Earvin would create a makeshift basketball out of anything available, usually his brothers' or sisters' socks. Anything was fair game as a basketball and the socks would turn up in the strangest places. That, too, drove Mrs. Johnson crazy.

The Main Street courts became Earvin's home away from home. He began playing as often as he could, sometimes getting up early enough to shoot around before school. In the summer it was morning till night; in winter it often meant shoveling the snow off the courts to make them playable. Nothing was too difficult when it came to finding ways to play.

He also got help from his three brothers. Older brother Larry was a particularly tough challenge for Earvin. They would play one-on-one, but not in the conventional way. The two of them went full court, pressing each other from baseline to baseline. That meant you learned to dribble if you wanted to survive. Otherwise, the ball would simply be stripped away from you.

"When Earvin first started getting up and going to play early, we would wonder where he was," said Mrs. Johnson. "I finally had to tell him not ever to leave home without telling us where he was going. After that he would always wake me up around daybreak to tell me he was going up to the courts."

It was at the Main Street courts that Earvin first developed what he called his "hoopsy doopsy" style. The courts were a popular place, crowded with youngsters looking to get into action. That meant court time was a premium item to be cherished and it was important to find the best way to stay there.

"Because the place was always packed with guys wanting to play, the only way you could hold the court was to keep winning," Magic said. "For that reason we always went for the hoop and the sure two instead of popping long outside shots."

His penchant to go to the hoop would remain a life-long court habit and one that would serve him well in later years. About that time he also found an unofficial coach and advisor. Though his father wasn't around much, he liked to spend some quality time with all his children. Earvin, Sr., loved drag racing and often took the boys to the track, which was located about 20 miles outside of town. Eventually he just took young Earvin because his daughters weren't interested and the older boys were already going in their own directions.

But once Mr. Johnson saw how much his son loved basketball, he began sharing his own knowledge of the game with him. Earvin, Sr., had played in high school, and while he never went further with the sport, he never lost his love for it and often watched pro games on television. Before long, father and son had a Sunday ritual. They would sit together and watch the NBA in action.

"My father would point things out to me as we watched," Magic said, "things like a big guard taking a smaller guard underneath, or guys running a pick-and-roll. By the time I started playing organized ball, whenever the coach asked if anybody knew how to do a three-man weave or a left-handed layup, I was always the first one up."

By the time Earvin was in the sixth grade he was starting to grow. Being taller than most of the other kids was an advantage. Being talented as well as tall was an even bigger advantage. And once he knew he had talent he began practicing in earnest, honing his ball-handling and shooting skills. He was already six feet tall when he entered Dwight Rich Junior High as a seventh grader. A year later he was 6'4" and by the time he was in the ninth grade had inched up to 6'5". That, alone, made him a coming star.

One of the byproducts of his incipient stardom was increasing notoriety, some of it formal, some of it of the schoolyard variety. As a standout performer on the Rich Junior High School team, Earvin began finding his name in the local papers. He was the team's high scorer and already a player who could do everything. He was tall enough to play center, could shoot and rebound with the skills of a forward, and he handled the ball with more than enough dexterity to operate at guard. The "hoopsy-doopsy" style learned on the Main Street playground kept him going to the hoop for those easy twos.

As in most cities, there was an out-of-school reputation to uphold as well. Earvin traveled from playground to playground taking on the best Lansing had to offer. The games were tough and the battle for top gun fought over and over again. The result was better ballplayers. By then the only player Earvin's age who could keep up with him in Lansing was Jay Vincent and the two of them battled constantly, both on the playgrounds and in the schools.

It was a classic rivalry, typical of inner-city basketball where reputations are won and lost on the concrete courts almost daily. Both Earvin and Jay Vincent had the same kind of drive and desire to be the best. Their rivalry sometimes moved beyond the basketball court. If they couldn't play hoops it might be pool, football, or even bowling. They were extremely competitive and they both wanted to win.

Learning that lesson early would be an asset Earvin Johnson would carry with him wherever he went. If Dwight Rich Junior High School was his first showcase,

Everett High School would become his first stage. He was about to enter a new world, just a step away from the big time. But before he climbed to the next plateau he would undergo a kind of transformation that would set the tone for all that would follow. Earvin Johnson would find himself christened *Magic*.

CHAPTER TWO

High School and a Heavy Choice

WHILE HE WAS STILL IN THE NINTH grade, Earvin met a man who would have a great influence on his life. His name was Dr. Charles Tucker and he was a psychologist with the Lansing School District. Dr. Tucker was a black man who was born in the south but grew up in Michigan. A fine student-athlete, Dr. Tucker played basketball at Western Michigan University while earning a master's degree in psychology.

Despite his intellectual bent, the lure of the court game was something Charles Tucker couldn't shake. He tried out for a number of pro teams and actually had a short stint with the old Memphis Tams of the now defunct American Basketball Association. He even played in the Continental League for several years while still clinging to his dream of making it in the NBA. But at the same time he never gave up his study of psychology, returning to Western Michigan and finally earning his doctorate.

Dr. Tucker made a professional visit to Rich Junior High to speak with the graduating class about their ultimate responsibilities to society. After school, he made a not-so-formal visit to the basketball courts outside the school. Within minutes he had doffed his coat and tie, and emerged in sweats and sneakers. It wasn't quite a Clark Kent to Superman transition, but in a matter of minutes Dr. Tucker was challenging Earvin Johnson to a game of one-on-one.

Not one to back down from a challenge, Earvin jumped in. He quickly found that his adversary knew every trick in the book, the little nuances of the game that can give a player the edge he sometimes needs. Dr. Tucker knew how to use his body on defense to hook, push, bump, and tug. On defense, he would position himself in such a way as to control Earvin's offensive moves. What he did was often subtle, but once his opponent had the grasp of it he could work to defeat it. He showed the youngster that there was a lot to learn. In fact, when Earvin questioned some of his tactics, he simply asked him if he wanted to learn the pro game. Earvin nodded and Dr. Tucker said he would be back the very next day.

Charles Tucker would serve as a coach, friend, and unofficial advisor in the years to come. Like many others, he must have seen something special in this tall youngster, something more than simply basketball talent. A lot of kids have talent; a rare few develop it to its ultimate. And fewer yet rise to the top of their profession with that talent.

The next step for Earvin Johnson was high school, three important and formative years when boys and

girls mature physically, emotionally, and psychologically. What they do and how they grow from the 10th to
12th grade often determines what the future will hold.
Earvin was looking forward to attending Sexton High,
which was located very close to his Middle Street home.
He had already been a frequent visitor to the school,
going to many football and basketball games. He often
watched the basketball team practice and was already
known to most of the players and the coach. The school
had a fine basketball team, a team that the 6'5" and
growing Earvin Johnson would undoubtedly help.

Because of its location in Lansing, Sexton High was
a predominately black school. However, in the social
climate of the mid-1970s there was a phenomena called
"forced bussing" which someone decided would be a
good experience for all involved. It meant taking a
group of students and bussing them to a school far
from their own neighborhood. The purpose of the bussing was to create a more equal racial and socio-econom-
ic mix at the schools. Instead, it often created animosity
and sometimes violence. The losers often turned out to
be the kids, who had to attend high school under
rather stressful conditions.

Shortly before he was to begin high school, Earvin
learned he would not be going to Sexton High. He lived
just outside the cutoff point for Sexton and instead
would be bussed to the predominately white Everett
High, some 15 minutes away. It was not welcome news
in the Johnson household. Earvin was upset because all
his good friends would be at Sexton. Even his parents
didn't like the idea, but they told him he had to obey
the law, and this was the law at the time.

There was some precedent for Earvin's trepidation.
Two of his older brothers, Quincy and Larry, had been
bussed to Everett before him. Both had been unhappy
there and had rather disturbing experiences. It was the

hardest for Quincy. He was at Everett at the start of the bussing experiment, when there were fights, brick throwing, and racist actions that almost led to riots. By the time Larry went there, the violence had ended, but when he was dropped from the basketball team, it was the unkindest cut of all. The coach, George Fox, didn't think Larry was good enough. Larry wondered if the cut wasn't racially motivated. So he, too, was unhappy there.

Enter brother number three. Larry didn't even want Earvin to try out for the team because of his own experience, but that was one favor Earvin couldn't grant. He had to play basketball. And there was also no question whatsover of George Fox cutting this Johnson from the team. He saw right away that he had a player of tremendous talent, a kid he could build the team around for three years.

The only problem was with some of the returning starters. They just weren't used to playing with someone as talented as Earvin Johnson. Very few high school players were capable of taking down a rebound at one end, dribbling the length of the court, and then going right at the hoop, either putting on a super move or dishing off at the last second to an open teammate. But Earvin was doing it with regularity. In other words, this incoming sophomore was already taking over the team.

There was some early resentment that resulted in a partial freezeout from teammates who wouldn't pass the ball to an open Johnson. When one senior did this with regularity, Earvin finally challenged him and the ensuing shouting match led to some rather nasty racial epithets being exchanged. When Coach Fox only partially defended Earvin because he was trying to keep his team intact, Earvin was ready to quit. It took his friend, Dr. Tucker, to mollify the situation. He explained to Earvin that the older boys weren't used to playing with someone as good and as talented as he was. They were simply frustrated that he was coming in and taking over the team.

Coach Fox, too, had to abandon some of his conservative ways and understand that the no-look pass, the airborne pass, and some of Earvin's other moves were both natural and effective, not forced and flashy. Pretty soon the resentment disappeared, the team began coming together and the coach was already bragging about his sophomore sensation.

"I got a kid here who's going to make believers out of everybody," he told the other coaches in the conference. "He's going to be the greatest player you ever saw."

By the time the 1974–75 season opened, Earvin had patched up the differences with his new teammates. Everett won its opening game by a single point, but without much help from the gangly, 6'5" sophomore. For one of the few times in his basketball life, Earvin Johnson had a case of the jitters and was tight. Coach Fox even had to listen to some of his friends tell him that he had overrated the youngster.

"Just wait," the coach said, confidently.

He was right. Beginning with the very next game Everett had a superstar, a player capable of taking over a game and controlling it at both ends of the floor. Earvin's new teammates quickly realized that it was more fun winning than losing and that this tall, thin sophomore with the long arms and legs was making them all better players.

By midseason, Everett High was considered one of the better teams in the area, a potential powerhouse, and the fifteen-year-old sophomore was beginning to astound more and more people with his precocious play. In a game against Jackson Parkside, Earvin rang up the kind of numbers that would soon become synonymous with the kind of all-court game he played. Everett won big as he led the way with 36 points, 18 rebounds and 16 assists. It wouldn't be until years later when this trio of stats became known as the "triple double." Back in the winter of 1974–75, it was simply a breathtaking, all-around performance.

On this particular night, however, there would be a special significance to those numbers. His breathtaking performance against Jackson Parkside would result in Earvin Johnson being tagged with one of the most identifiable nicknames in the history of sport. It happened after the game when the local reporters gathered around to get a word or two from the game's star. Earvin was quickly getting used to being the center of post-game attention. In fact, he rather enjoyed it.

When the reporters had just about finished, Earvin noticed a young man named Fred Stabley, who wrote for the *Lansing State Journal*, standing toward the back of the pack and poring over his notes. Finally, when the others left, Stabley approached him. First he congratulated Earvin on a great game. Then he said, without hesitation and as if he had been thinking about it for a long time: "I've got to give you a nickname. Is that all right with you?"

Earvin had no objections. He knew that Stabley had the entire scenerio planned when the young reporter quickly dismissed two obvious ones.

"You can't be Doctor J or the Big E," Stabley said. "They're both taken." He was referring, of course, to Julius Erving and Elvin Hayes, two great professional players. Then, after a moment's pause in which he seemed to be working up the courage to spring his idea, he said, "Can I call you Magic?"

Earvin thought a minute, said the name to himself several times and then nodded his approval. He liked the sound of it, thought he would later admit it embarrassed him somewhat at first. But Fred Stabley wasted no time introducing it to readers of the *Lansing State Journal*. In his game story the next day he referred to the Everett star as Earvin "Magic" Johnson. It would be difficult to find another nickname anywhere that has the kind of universal recognition that would come to "Magic" Johnson.

Of course, that didn't happen overnight. Earvin's father thought at first that the nickname might put too much pressure on his son, that people would actually expect him to perform magic on the basketball court. And Earvin himself heard his share of catcalls from the stands. Everyone wanted to know who Magic was. But the pressure never bothered him. Put pressure on him, challenge him, dare him to be great, and he would respond. Even then.

Oddly enough, his teammates rarely used the nickname. To them he was plain Earvin, or E.J., and sometimes E. Years later, when he was dazzling the world with the Lakers, Coach Riley and his teammates still didn't favor the moniker which, by then, was universal. To them he was just Earvin or sometimes Buck, another nickname he acquired. But to the public he was Magic and always would be. It caught on and everyone loved it.

Magic's best friend on the team was a junior guard named Reggie Chastine. Reggie stood just 5'3" and made a startling constrast to his tall friend. They must have looked strange hanging out together and not surprisingly were given the tag of Mutt and Jeff.

The team finished the season at 22–2. It was the second defeat, however, that was the heartbreaker. It came against Dearborn Fordson in the quarterfinals of the state tournament. The tough part was that Everett had a 13-point lead in the final quarter and missed a slew of foul shots to let the game slip away. Magic cried after that one. Losing was never easy. But for a fifteen-year-old playing in his first state tournament, it was an especially tough burden to bear. With all his heroics, Earvin Johnson was also quick to accept blame when things didn't go as expected.

Not surprisingly, Magic was an all-city and second team all-state selection as a sophomore. That was one reason his reputation began to spread. The other reason was Earvin himself. His policy starting from junior high days was to look for the best players around and compete with them. The better the guy you're up against, he felt, the more you'll learn. The more you learn, the better you get. It was a simple formula, but it sometimes involved taking a chance and putting that rep squarely on the line.

One summer, for instance, while he was at Everett he traveled to Rocky Mount, North Carolina, with his family to visit relatives. Naturally, the first thing Magic did was look for a basketball court. It didn't take long for the local kids to see the visitor was a talented player. Sure enough, in a matter of minutes there was a challenge. It came from a twenty-year-old who was supposedly as good as Phil Ford, who also came from Rocky Mount and was then starring at the University of North Carolina.

Not one to pass up a challenge, Magic accepted. The two would play to fifteen baskets with a twenty dollar bet on the outcome of the game. The local guy started off hot. He made six straight baskets before Magic could manage to score. His friends were having a grand old time, laughing it up on the sidelines. But none of them knew Earvin Johnson.

Suddenly, Earvin turned into Magic and began dominating the action. The older boy couldn't cope with his spinning moves to the basket, shades of "hoopsy-doopsy" days back home. When he backed off to stop the drive, Magic simply popped a jump shot. After his 6–0 start, the local guy scored just two more hoops as the kid from Lansing blew him out.

"The guy was really upset," recalled Magic. "He even tried to get his friends to lend him more money so he could play me again. But they had seen enough. They just wouldn't do it."

Magic also used to hang out at the IM Building where the Michigan State players often worked out during the off-season. In fact, he started going up there while he was still in the ninth grade. That's when he met Terry Furlow, who was then the Michigan State star and later played in the NBA. Furlow was a jump-shot artist who loved to bomb from long range. Believe it or not, Magic was playing one-on-one against Furlow before he even reached Everett High. He didn't win, but he learned.

"The first time I went up there it was just to watch," Magic said. "Then Terry picked me to play with him and I was scared. But then he started calling me his main man and bragging on me. I never forgot that."

Terry Furlow, incidentally, became the top draft choice of the Philadelphia 76ers in 1976 and played four years in the NBA before losing his life in a car accident in the spring of 1980. By that time, Furlow was fighting a battle with drugs. Magic learned from that, as well.

He also played against other NBA stars such as George Gervin, Campy Russell, and Ben Poquette. Gervin, a 6'7" guard known as the Iceman, was an NBA scoring champion and amazed Magic with the variety of smooth offensive moves he had. Magic always thought "Ice" was one of the best.

Still another time Magic ran into his arch-rival, Jay Vincent, at an outdoor concert during the summer. Before long the two boys were talking basketball, their favorite topic. During an intermission at the concert they headed over to the basketball courts to see if there was any action. Naturally, there was a game in progress between some older boys who had been high school stars in town a few years earlier. When the game ended, the two winners looked around and immediately pointed toward Johnson and Vincent. It was a challenge that could not be refused.

The two high-schoolers proceeded to give the older boys a basketball lesson. They were so spectacular that it didn't take long for more and more people to come over to the courts as the word spread. Magic and Jay Vincent were incredible. They both dunked repeatedly, hit jumpers, whipped quick passes between them and ran the two older boys into the ground. After that day, no boys in Lansing would ever play against the tandem of Johnson and Vincent again.

So it was quickly becoming a complete basketball life for Magic. He was a good student who made sure his grades stayed up, but basketball was the thing that really got the juices flowing. Once his sophomore season ended, he began working toward his junior year. He hadn't forgotten the crushing loss in the state tournament. Winning the state championship quickly became his goal. He had grown another inch to 6'6" and was beginning to fill out. Coach Fox made a big decision that year, too. He decided to move Magic to point guard to take full advantage of his many and varied skills.

Operating at the point, Magic quickly became the talk of the town. It was a rarity even in the pros to see a point guard as tall as Magic. But in high school such a thing was practically unheard of. Where would a kid of sixteen in the midst of a growth spurt—a period when many fast-growing boys go through an awkward and clumsy stage—acquire the skills and the poise to play point guard? That meant handling the ball against smaller, quicker boys, breaking the press, dribbling through traffic and passing off to cutting teammates. Magic did it all with ease.

He already had total court vision, an innate sense of where his teammates were and where they would be seconds later. His ball-handling skills had been honed by hours on the playgrounds and by constantly competing against better players whenever and wherever he could find them. Now, all the hard work, combined with his natural aptitude for the game, was paying off. Oh yes, if all else failed and he was trapped, he was tall enough to simply pass the ball over the outstretched arms of the defenders.

Magic truly was magic his junior year. He led Everett to a one-loss season and back into the state tournament. Then, for the second year in a row, it all slipped away. This time it was in the semi-finals against Catholic Central of Detroit. Everett led by five at the half and then lost the game after intermission. Once again Magic took the blame. He felt he had played it too conservatively and, in a basketball sense, was simply not selfish enough.

"I didn't assert myself enough and go to the hoop," he said. "Instead I kept passing off because I wanted to get everyone on the team into the offense."

As devastating as a big loss can be, it's something that can eventually be handled. It's not as easy for a youngster as it is for a pro. But sooner or later everyone learns that no one can win them all. For a kid of sixteen, there will be many more games, many additional titles to be won, many chances to be the hero . . . or the goat. But when you're sixteen and eliminated from the state championship tournament for the second year in a row, it has to feel like the end of the world.

A different kind of reality hit home that summer

when Magic learned that his good friend, Reggie Chastine, had been killed in an automobile accident. That kind of loss was devastating and permanent. All the boys on the Everett team dedicated the following season to their former teammate. And for Earvin Johnson, losses on the basketball court had a slightly lesser overall significance from that point on.

The 1976–77 season, however, had to be the most exciting time of Earvin Johnson's young life. He had become a thoroughly dominating high school basketball player and, as trite as it might sound, about as close to a one-man team as anyone could get. In addition, he was far from being a secret and the college recruiters were beginning to pop out from under every bush and around every corner. Fortunately, Magic had a strong support group to help keep everything in perspective. There were his parents, Charles Tucker, Coach Fox, and even the principal at Everett, Dr. Frank Throop.

In fact, it was Dr. Throop's office that served as a stopping point for everyone and anyone trying to reach Magic. To allow recruiters to have open access to any young man is dangerous and wrong. Too many shady deals can be cut and empty promises made, not to mention the sometimes subtle, sometimes overt, violations of the stringent NCAA recruiting rules. A young man who has let high school success fill his head with images of self-importance is most prone to falling into the trap. In other words, the kids with the swelled heads and cocky attitudes most often make the mistakes.

Fortunately for Earvin Johnson, this never happened. Neither his parents or Dr. Tucker would allow it. His nickname might have been Magic, but he always knew there were no tricks and no shortcuts. Things had to be done right and he was determined not to make any major mistakes, on or off the court, his senior year.

On the court, he *was* magic. The added maturity, the physical growth, the honing of his skills made him virtually unstoppable. It was like a man playing against boys. Over the first several games of the season, it was truly the Magic Show. He was scoring between thirty and forty points a game, no easy feat when you consider a high school game is just thirty-two minutes long. In fact, in one contest he exploded for a career best of fifty-four. The team was winning and Magic had the incredible feeling that he could do whatever he wanted on the court. What followed, however, was another example of the character in the heart of Earvin Johnson.

Coach Fox called him into his office one day shortly before Christmas and basically asked him to tone his game down. "You're doing too much out there," he told a surprised Magic.

What the coach meant was that Magic's skills were so overwhelming and dominating that his teammates were just standing around and watching him do his thing. They were barely involved with the offense. In effect, they were almost as intimidated by Magic's presence as was the opposition. The coach voiced his concern that if and when the time came for the others to contribute more in order to win a game, they might not be ready.

Enough said. While another superstar player with a different kind of ego might have been reluctant to divert the spotlight from himself, Magic didn't hesitate. The next time out he made an abrupt change in his game. Once again he made sure to pass out the goodies, setting his teammates up for high-percentage shots with his timely and accurate passes. While his scoring totals dropped, Everett High continued to win and looked like a much stronger team in the process.

By the time Everett met Eastern High with Jay

Vincent, they were unbeaten and ranked number one in the state. Eastern, however, was number two. The game was so big it was played at the Jenison Field House on the Michigan State campus before nearly 10,000 fans. It was an Eastern day. Vincent's team took an early lead and held it throughout to hand Magic and his teammates a crushing defeat.

But then Eastern lost a game the very next week and because of that the two ballclubs met again in the first round of the district playoffs. The game was played in the Eastern gym and was televised locally. Because they were playing at home, Eastern was the slight favorite. But Coach Fox and his star devised a game plan that would utilize their greatest strength while at the same time taking away Eastern's. It worked.

Offensively, Everett jumped into a quick lead, then spread the offense. This allowed Magic to be isolated on a defender where he could take advantage of the one-on-one situation. He could either go to the hoop, pull up for a jumper, or dish off to a teammate. The spread allowed him to take complete control of the offense. At the same time, Everett played a collapsing defense that surrounded Jay Vincent every time he put the ball on the floor and started to make a move. He was held to just a single field goal and a pair of free throws. Everett won easily.

From there Magic and his teammates achieved their longtime goal. They went all the way to the finals, then beat a very good Brother Rice team from Birmingham, Michigan, in overtime to become state champs. At last. Magic was the toast of the town and a consensus high school All-American. It was obvious to everyone around him just what he would do for an encore. The only question was where would he do it?

*   *   *

Earvin Johnson had been getting letters from recruiters dating back to his sophomore year. It didn't take him long to realize that basketball was his ticket to college. But there was no way he could have realized then what a wildly frenetic process it would become. There's simply no way a potential recruit and his family can handle this kind of thing alone, especially if the youngster was as talented as Earvin Johnson had become.

It seemed as if nearly every school in the country with a basketball program sent out some kind of feeler to Earvin. The majority of these schools were well aware they had virtually no chance of getting him, not when he had carte blanche and could make his own choice. Knowing Magic's competitive nature and his desire to play against the best, it was clear that he would go to a Division I school.

College recruiting can be a rather insidious process. Unfortunately, not all recruiters follow the rules, and even those who do can be aggressive to the point of harassment. It isn't unusual for recruiters to call a prospect's home very late at night or extremely early in the morning. Sometimes they will appear on the doorstep uninvited, like an persistent salesman who refuses to waver until he has made his pitch. And even then they won't take no for an answer. Recruiters have taken hotel rooms in the town or neighborhood where the prospect lives, hoping to talk to him as much as they can and simply not leaving until a decision is made.

Then there are the promises and the illegal perks. It's no secret that there is an under-the-table world in college recruiting. The NCAA does what it can to curb it, but the practice is as old as recruiting itself. Youngsters from poor or impoverished backgrounds are often considered easy prey. The temptation of a new car, a color television for their parents or simply cold cash is sometimes hard to resist. And that's why every prime recruit should have that solid support group, people he can trust, people who are not looking to line their own pockets on the coattails of his talent.

In that respect, Magic was lucky, almost blessed. The people around him wanted what was best for him, no more, no less. But that still didn't mean the entire recruiting process was easy. There was one recruiter from an Atlantic Coast Conference school who had to be barred from the grounds of Everett High during school hours. He had been staying in Lansing and was trying to talk to Magic at every turn.

Others tried to get to Magic by calling the house and sweet-talking his mother. After all, if you can get the mother on your side, it's assumed she has a great deal of influence with the son. Anyone who began with the under-the-table promises, however, was eliminated immediately. Charles Tucker saw to that. He told Magic that he was good enough to get the things he wanted on his own and it would be foolish to risk that future for what seemed like a quick fix.

At that time, recruits were allowed to make visits to six college campuses. Magic made only four. They were Maryland, Notre Dame, North Carolina, and Michigan. The fifth visit would have been to Michigan State. But the campus was practically down the road in East Lansing and Magic had virtually grown up there, having already spent more time on the basketball courts there than many of the Spartan players.

The potential sixth trip is an interesting story. Not surprisingly, one of the schools high on Magic's list was the University of California at Los Angeles, the famed UCLA. From 1964 to 1975, the Bruins under Coach John Wooden won ten NCAA championships in the most dominating show of college hoop power in history. It seemed like the campus at Westwood was a gathering place for all-Americans year after year. The names are still well remembered—Goodrich, Hazzard, Alcindor, Allen, Warren, Rowe, Wicks, Bibby, Walton, Wilkes, and Marques Johnson. Nearly all of the above went on to star in the pros. Lew Alcindor, of course, would later change his name to Kareem Abdul-Jabbar. With that kind of tradition, it was no wonder that a wide-eyed kid from Lansing would be interested.

So a visit to the campus was arranged by an assistant coach for the Bruins. Magic admits that he was excited and looking forward to the trip for several months. Then a week before the trip was to take place, Magic got a call from the coach claiming there had been a scheduling mix-up. Apparently a player from New York, Albert King, was going to be visiting on the weekend that was supposed to be Magic's. So he was asked to pick a weekend later in the year.

Magic and his advisors were annoyed. "It's now or never," they told the people at UCLA. But the answer was that it simply couldn't be arranged that quickly. When a player is told the school cannot make any accommodations to get him to the campus, he begins to feel they don't really want him very much. Magic admitted to being insulted by the way UCLA handled the situation. He immediately crossed the Bruins off his list. Albert King, by the way, ended up at Maryland.

Maryland was also one of the five schools remaining in the Johnson sweepstakes. The others were Michigan, Michigan State, Notre Dame, and North Carolina. Now the recruiting pace picked up. As Magic said, the decision was becoming a constant "tug of war" with everybody trying to sway him one way or another.

His father openly favored Michigan State, because it was so close to home. But at the same time he kept telling Magic it was his call, that he was old enough to make up his own mind. Easier said than done. Recruiting can be a wearing and wearying process. At first it strokes the ego. Hey, all these people want me! I'm the center of attention. But when it continues week after week, month after month, it quickly becomes an old record that needs changing.

"Too many phony smiles, insincere speeches, and illegal offers," was the way Magic put it.

His goal even then was to play in the NBA. While always a good student and conscientious about his studies, Magic's main concern was basketball. He knew he was pro material and his passion for the court game had never wavered. No matter where he went he would continue to work to keep his grades up. Options had to remain open, because athletic careers can end at any time. Just one misstep, one wrong landing after a leap, a teammate or opponent in the wrong place and a ballplayer can blow out a knee. Like every player, Earvin Johnson was aware of this. If something unforeseen happened to sabotage his basketball career, he knew he would have to find something else.

But if all went well, it would be basketball. He had to laugh when one recruiter went into a long speech about his school's programs in biochemistry and nuclear research. Though far from the stereotype dumb jock, even then there was no pretense about Magic Johnson. What you saw was what you got. His expressive face was always an open book, showing joy, sorrow, elation, disappointment—often all during the course of a single game. But biochemistry and nuclear research! That wasn't in the Magic man's plans. To even discuss it with him was plain silly.

Toward the end of his senior year, Magic began eliminating schools one by one. Notre Dame and North Carolina were lopped off the list. Then Maryland. It was now apparent that Earvin Johnson would not be leaving his home state. It would be either Michigan or Michigan State.

The familiarity and closeness of State made it the early favorite. Although the Michigan campus at Ann Arbor was only about fifty miles from Lansing, Magic already considered Michigan State a kind of home away from home. He revealed that even during his junior year, Michigan State was number one. By that time he knew and liked the Spartans' coach, Gus Ganakas. It didn't matter that State didn't have the basketball reputation that Michigan had. Heck, if Magic could dust off UCLA because they didn't go out of their way to get him to the campus, then it was obvious he wasn't worried about the basketball reputations of the competing schools.

However, after Magic's junior year at Everett, Gus Ganakas was released and replaced by Jud Heathcote, an expressively emotional coach with something of a reputation as a screamer. The coaching change caused Magic to once again reconsider his options.

Then, a short time after Everett won the state championship, Magic joined a group of select high school seniors to play at the Albert Schweitzer Games in West Germany. Being away gave him time to reflect and also perform with a powerful all-star team that went undefeated against teams from eight other countries. Five other players on that team—Tracy Jackson, Darnell Valentine, Eddie Johnson, Jeff Lamp, and Jeff Ruland—went on to play in the NBA.

But when Magic returned to Michigan he wasn't ready for the reception he found waiting for him at the Lansing Airport. As he left the plane he saw a large crowd bisected into two distinct groups. Both held identical banners that read WELCOME HOME, MAGIC. It took a few seconds for Magic to realize what the two groups represented. One was from Michigan

State, the other from Michigan. Both had inadvertently reopened the recruiting war before Magic was even down the steps of the plane.

There was no longer any way to avoid it. Earvin Johnson knew that push had come to shove. He had to make a decision and make it soon.

CHAPTER

THREE

The Spartan Years

THE DECISION CAME WITHIN THREE DAYS of Magic's return from West Germany. All those closest to him said they would support his decision, no matter what it was. As always, Magic's goal was to win and to take that as far as was possible, to win the NCAA championship. There was little doubt that Michigan had the stronger program. Michigan State had only been 10–17 the season before, the first under Jud Heathcote. Again it was Charles Tucker who was the voice of reason and balance.

Dr. Tucker told Magic that he shouldn't pick Michigan solely because they had the better basketball program. He said there was also talent at Michigan State and that Magic could win there.

"If you think you're that good, then you make the program," Dr. Tucker told Magic.

That might have done it. A press conference was hastily arranged and Magic told his family that he would be attending Michigan State. He would later explain his final choice this way: "Michigan thought it had a lot more to offer than Michigan State. And it did. The Wolverines were on national TV a lot more than State, things like that. But I liked the underdog school. I've always been the underdog. Every team I've been on wasn't supposed to win. Even when I go to the playgrounds I don't necessarily pick the best players. I always pick the players who want to work hard."

Magic wasn't the only star in Lansing to choose Michigan State. Old rival Jay Vincent also decided to stay at home. Plus the Spartans already had a fine forward named Greg Kelser who had great speed and jumping ability. He would be a junior in 1977–78. Now the school had recruited its point guard. He was 6'8" and weighed in the neighborhood of 200 pounds. Showtime, Michigan State style, was about to begin.

At the press conference, Magic was his usual upbeat, ebullient self.

"When it came down to making a decision, I don't think I could have gone anywhere else," he told the large gathering. "I was born to be a Spartan."

His loyalties already firmly in place, Magic then made a brash prediction when someone reminded him that he would be attending a school that didn't have much of a basketball reputation.

"I don't care about what happened in the past or about reputations," he said. "All I care about is the future, and I see an NCAA championship for Michigan State."

Once he hit the campus Magic was an instant hit. With his bright smile and friendly demeanor, he became a favorite with the student body. Since his reputation had preceded him—and was established just down the road—everyone was anxious to meet him. Magic lit up the East Lansing campus the same way he would light up the basketball court.

Though home was close by, Magic moved into a campus dorm and roomed with his friend and former rival, Jay Vincent. He chose telecommunications as a major and already talked about going into television announcing once his playing days were ended. Basketball practice didn't begin right away, but Magic wasn't one to waste any time. He attended class faithfully and cracked the books hard. Knowing how much of his time and energy would be required during basketball season, he wanted to lay down a sound academic foundation. He also became a part-time disc jockey at a campus disco, billing himself as E.J. the DeeJay.

But once basketball started, E.J. the DeeJay was again transformed into Magic and the word began spreading quickly that this Spartan team was going to be decidedly different from past versions. Michigan State was not considered a "basketball" school. Football remained the major sport, with hoops always playing a secondary role. But the football team had recently been hit with some NCAA sanctions, so the arrival of Magic Johnson came at just the right time.

In fact, the box office at the 9,886-seat Jenison Field House was opened the day after Magic announced he was coming and in two hours 100 season tickets were gobbled up. Tickets continued to sell briskly and by the time the team was set to open, there was a sellout. And by that time, everyone was anxious to see this 6'8" whirlwind perform his magic. Maybe his father had been right. With a nickname like Magic, people expected an awful lot.

Not surprisingly, both Magic and Jay Vincent would

be starting in the 1977–78 opener against Western Michigan. The two top returnees were Kelser and guard Bob Chapman. With just those four players alone, Coach Heathcote had the nucleus of a winning team. Oddly enough, Magic had the same kind of butterflies before his first collegiate game as he had before his first contest at Everett. He was nervous and tight, and it showed.

After a thunderous standing ovation when he was introduced, he went out and looked like anything but an innovative court superstar. He was rather ordinary, scoring just seven points. He did add nine rebounds and eight assists, but those weren't the kinds of numbers Magic's fans were accustomed to seeing. Fortunately, Jay Vincent had a 25-point debut and the others players were solid, allowing the Spartans to come from behind and win the game.

But as had been the case at Everett, the jitters lasted for just a single night. Once past that hurdle, Magic began doing his thing and in the eyes of many, doing it better than any other guard in the country. For openers, most people just couldn't believe that a 6'8" point guard could run a fast-breaking offense with as much or more efficiency as a quick, smaller man. Even though the evolution of the game had produced bigger and stronger players at every position, 6'8" players were still looked upon as potential power forwards in the college game.

Yet once the Spartans began winning big and in spectacular fashion, more and more reporters and writers flocked to East Lansing to get a closer look at this phenomenon called Magic Johnson. In fact, at one point early in the season, Magic apologized to his teammates because of the amount of attention and publicity he was receiving. He didn't want it to become disruptive or cause the team to lose focus.

That wasn't happening. Vincent was proving a solid

player at center, though he wasn't overly tall at 6'8", the same size as his point-guard teammate. But the player Magic seemed to work best with was Greg Kelser. Kelser was a jumping jack with a superb sense of timing around the hoop. Magic spotted that quickly and before long the two were dazzling opponents and spectators with a series of flying slam-dunks. Kelser would break to the hoop, and leap high in the air near the hoop. At the height of his jump he'd reach up and Magic would have the ball right there. All Kelser had to do was catch it and slam it home.

Though Kelser was also extremely talented, it was Magic who was making the play and getting the raves. Even opposing coaches, used to handling Michigan State without much trouble over the years, suddenly wondered where this bolt of lightning offense had come from. It didn't take them long to find out. All they had to do was watch the ball. It was usually in the hands of number 33, the most exciting freshman player in the country.

By early January the Spartans were 12–1, an amazing turn-around from the losing season a year earlier. They were getting close to the top ten and already embarking on their Big Ten Conference schedule. Michigan State hadn't won a conference crown since 1959 and the fans were hungry. With the numbers Magic and his teammates were running up, the Big Ten title seemed a definite possibility.

"We hoped Earvin could come in and be a contributing player," Coach Heathcote said. "Instead, he has been one of our dominant players. He brings an enthusiasm onto the court that's contagious, and he always plays to win."

Heathcote wasn't the only one who noticed. Magic was beginning to put together a string of outstanding performances. He had thirty-one points in a win over

Minnesota, adding eight rebounds and four assists. He also made a clutch thirteen of fifteen from the free throw line. Two nights later the Spartans whipped Wisconsin as he scored eighteen, grabbed seven boards and handed off for six assists. Those two performances made him Big Ten Player of the Week.

But there were other big nights. Against Wichita State he had nineteen points, twenty rebounds and nine assists. Illinois got a taste of Magic to the tune of seventeen points, ten assists, eight rebounds and four steals. He was playing a tremendous all-around game and was undoubtedly the best rebounding point guard in the nation, maybe in the world. The plaudits were rolling in from everywhere.

"He's great," said Lou Henson, the Illinois coach. "I haven't seen a 6'8" freshman who can do the things he can do."

A former high school rival, Kevin Smith, who was a freshman at the University of Detroit that year, thought Earvin Johnson had the perfect nickname.

"I'm not surprised at anything he does," said Smith, "because he *is* magic. There's no question he's a special person. He draws people to him like a magnet."

One thing he was drawing already were looks from the NBA. With the so-called hardship declaration, underclassmen were eligible for the draft. Most players who came out early were juniors, passing up their senior seasons for a shot at the brass ring . . . or more accurately, the green paper. Yet here was a freshman barely halfway through his first collegiate season and already the NBA was interested.

The first feeler came from the Kansas City Kings (now the Sacramento Kings), who contacted Magic's father to see if there was any interest.

"Johnson could start for anybody in the league tomorrow," said K.C. general manager Joe Axelson, in what had to be a supreme compliment for an 18-year-old freshman. "He's the most exciting college player I've ever seen. I can't believe God created a 6'8" player who can handle the ball like that."

Purdue coach Fred Schaus echoed the sentiment by calling Magic the "finest freshman I've ever seen."

There's little doubt that Magic was flattered by the early NBA interest. He said he would consider it at the end of the season, but most of those around him felt there was very little chance of his going pro after just one year at State. But when large sums of money are dangled in front of a young man who has never had a lot of it before, anything can happen.

Magic had already shown he was a player who could adjust to situations. Because college players were better than most of his high school opponents, he couldn't freewheel as much with the basketball. Magic himself said that in high school he often went up in the air first, then looked to make the play second. He quickly learned he couldn't do this in college. It was too easy to be caught in the air with no place to go.

The other big adjustments. "More defeats," he said. "I had to adjust to the reality that we were going to lose a number of games. Now I didn't have as long and painful a recovery period."

But he didn't lose too many. With Magic controlling the offense, the Spartans ran their way to a school-record twenty-five victories. They finished the year at 25–5 and won the Big Ten title with a 15–3 conference mark. Johnson and Kelser were a great one–two punch. Kelser led the team in both scoring and rebounding, with Magic next. He averaged seventeen points a game, adding eight rebounds and seven assists, along with a forty-six percent shooting average from the field.

It wasn't the numbers that made him a unanimous All-Big-Ten choice or the only freshman to be named to a major All-American team. Rather it was his overall court presence and leadership.

"In Earvin's case you don't talk about the points he scores," said Jud Heathcote. "Rather, it's the points he produces. And that doesn't mean just the baskets and assists, but the first pass that makes the second pass possible. He's conscious of scoring himself, but it isn't an obsession with him. He doesn't worry about getting his average every game."

Magic, too, acknowledged that it was the intangibles, rather than the numbers, that made him able to direct a team and usually make it come out on top.

"My whole game is court sense," he said. "Being smart, taking charge, setting up a play or, if I have to, scoring. I've tried to pattern myself after George Gervin and Dr. J. I don't shoot the way they do, but they're both big, and they handle the ball and they're smooth."

As Big Ten champs, the Spartans automatically qualified for the NCAA tournament and there were some who felt the team had a chance to win it. They had little trouble beating Providence and Western Kentucky in their first two games. From there it was on to the Mideast Regional final against the Kentucky Wildcats, the top-ranked team in the country. If the Spartans could pull off the upset they would be in the Final Four.

Joe B. Hall's Wildcats were quite a contrast to the Spartans. They had a pair of 6'11" starters in center Mike Phillips and forward Rick Robey. The tallest Spartans were Vincent and Magic at 6'8". Wildcat point guard Kyle Macy was only 6'2" and not nearly strong enough to handle Magic. Forward Jack Givens might have been the quickest of the Wildcats, but he didn't have Kelser's speed. Some felt Magic and his teammates might be able to run the Wildcats into the ground. It was also felt that the winner of this one would be favored to go all the way.

Magic and his teammates were confident going in. They felt they had too much quickness for the bigger Kentucky team. Unfortunately, they never had a chance to really put the theory to a test. Though the Spartans held a five-point lead at the half, many thought it could have been more. The team seemed to be holding back, not running at every opportunity. For its part, Kentucky tried to slow the pace intentionally. They didn't want to get into a track meet with Magic and Greg Kelser.

In the second half things got even more curious. Suddenly, it was the Spartans playing a conservative game, slowing down when they could have been speeding up. It was as if they were playing right into the Wildcats' hands. Though the game remained close right to the end, it was Kentucky that finally prevailed, 52–49, and moved to the Final Four where a national championship was waiting.

The loss was a bitter pill for the Spartans to swallow. As Magic said, "We felt we had lost the game, not that Kentucky had won it."

No one felt worse than Coach Heathcote. It was his decision to slow the pace. Putting the reins on a group of antelopes is never a good idea. Maybe he felt his young team could hold on if the pace slowed. But as Magic said, it took the team out of its rhythm. Earvin Johnson was never one to walk the ball up-court.

Nevertheless, it had still been a much more successful season than anyone had envisioned. But the folks at East Lansing now had something to worry about. Everyone knew the NBA would be courting the team's star despite the fact that he had completed just one year in college. Magic was aware of it, too, because the Kansas City Kings had made the first contact with him at midseason. The Kings would have the first pick in the upcoming NBA draft and if he wanted to be eligible, Magic would have to declare hardship within a month.

Once again he had to play the game of pro and con, plus and minus, should I or shouldn't I? It was bad enough that just a year earlier he'd had to make a major choice of a college. Now, a year later, he was being asked to decide if he should leave that college or not. That's quite a burden to place on an eighteen-year-old, even one as athletically precocious as Magic Johnson.

What it came to was this: The argument to stay in school included an enjoyable campus life, the prospect of playing on a national championship team, the possibility of becoming College Player of the Year, being a consensus All-American and playing on the 1980 United States Olympic team.

The argument to leave school and turn pro was . . . money!

That wasn't quite the whole story. Magic's lifelong dream was to play in the NBA and he felt he was good enough to make the transition immediately. The devil's advocate might say, so what, if the money is there this year, it will surely be there the next, and probably more of it, especially if he had an even better season at Michigan State. The argument to counter that, of course, is what if he blew out a knee the next year with the Spartans? That could mean good-bye money forever.

So it wasn't an easy decision. Again. Magic's support group, however, was unanimous in feeling he should remain in school. His mother felt he was too young. Both his father and Charles Tucker questioned whether the time was right and wondered if he was really ready. Magic, though, admitted he was still drawn by the prospect of big dollars.

It came down to a meeting between Dr. Tucker and Magic, and Joe Axelson of the Kings. The annual salary the Kings were offering was in the $250,000 range along with a bonus and some guarantees. Magic and his good friend left the meeting with the anticipation of his returning to school. The Kings kept calling for the next few days, trying to work something out. But they didn't budge on the basic salary and before long the deadline to file hardship passed. To the relief of everyone in East Lansing, he would remain at Michigan State.

Once that decision was made, Magic could look forward to a busy summer of basketball. This time he played on a pair of all-star teams. One toured a number of southern states; the other went to Europe and Russia. The first club contained a number of outstanding college players such as Darrell Griffith, Phil Ford, Rick Robey, Kyle Macy, Sidney Moncrief and a guy named Larry Bird. It was the first time Magic had played alongside Larry and the two clicked immediately. Magic remembers coming downcourt on a three-on-two fastbreak, flipping a no-look pass to Bird, who never batted an eyelash before no-looking the ball back to Magic for an easy layup.

Both players must have thought how great it would be to play together on a regular basis. Each was a student of the game and knew how to play for both maximum excitement and effectiveness. What neither knew then, however, was how their collegiate and professional lives would be intertwined, beginning the very next year.

By all standards, the Spartans looked like an even better team in 1978–79. Magic, Jay Vincent, and Greg Kelser were all a year older and more mature. Forward-center Ron Charles, forward Mike Brkovich and guard Terry Donnelly were also fine ballplayers. Those six would see the bulk of the playing time. Once again the Spartans planned to run. The team didn't have a real big man and hopefully wouldn't make the same mistake it had made in the NCAA regionals against Kentucky the year before. They wouldn't slow it down against teams that had the horses up front.

The pre-season Associated Press poll had the Spartans ranked seventh nationally. Magic, of course, was their marquee player and it seemed his picture was everywhere. The team opened with a big 76–60 win over the Russian national team, then went on to three more over non-league opponents before being stopped by nationally ranked North Carolina, 70–69.

After that, the team won another six games, running its overall record to 10–1. The last two victories in the string were against Big Ten rivals Wisconsin and Minnesota. In both games, the Spartans made it look easy, winning 84–55 and 69–62. But then something happened. The Spartans were beaten by Illinois and Purdue, losing both games by two points. After solid victories over Indiana and Iowa, they then lost a one-point decision to Michigan and were upset by Northwestern, 83–65. That was a pretty good thrashing and also the Spartans' fourth loss in six games, evening their Big Ten record at 4–4. The sudden turn of events dropped the ballclub out of the top ten.

Losing was always the toughest thing for Magic to take, especially this way. For one thing, he couldn't remember being on a team that lost four of six games before. Secondly, it was looking almost as if the team was ready to fall apart. That, too, was something that had never happened to him when he was directing traffic on the floor. Later he would admit that a communications gap had opened up between Coach Heathcote and the players. He wasn't sure what to do about it.

Finally the coach called a team meeting and asked everyone to please speak up. There were problems. The ballclub wasn't rebounding well, the running game was out of sync and the team was once again doing what it had done against Kentucky in last year's regionals—sitting on a lead instead of going for the kill. They finally decided to go to an all-out running game, forty minutes worth each night, with the hope of salvaging the season and maybe still making it to the NCAA tournament.

What's surprising, looking back, is that they didn't do it sooner. They had the best guy available to run the show, a player capable of running the fast break from start to finish and running it with a flourish. The first game after the meeting was with Ohio State. The Buckeyes were the Big Ten leader with a perfect 8–0 slate. Running from start to finish, Michigan State drove Ohio State to distraction. Magic was at his best and the Spartans won, 84–79. They were back.

Nine more victories followed before the regular season ended with an 83–81 upset by Wisconsin. Michigan State finished regulation play with a 21–6 record overall and a 13–5 mark in conference play. That gave them a share of The Big Ten title and a second straight invitation to the NCAA championship. Once again, people were singing the praises of Earvin Johnson, beginning with his own coach.

"He's the best player in the open court today," said Jud Heathcote. "That includes a guy like Pete Maravich or anyone else you want to name. If Earvin stays in college all four years, he will be remembered as the one player who put the pass back into the game. Bob Cousy showed people the value of the pass on the fast break. Earvin is showing what it can do for an entire offense. And that's because his court vision is so tremendous."

Coach Heathcote was already equating Magic with a pair of all-time greats of the game. But he wasn't the only one. Earvin was an impact player who had really just begun to make his mark. In a real sense, the story was just beginning. In the few weeks following the end of the regular season, the next long chapter would begin to unfold. And through it all, Earvin "Magic" Johnson would never be very far from the spotlight. It was as if he belonged there.

CHAPTER FOUR

The Magic Man and the Bird Man

JUST FIVE MORE GAMES. THAT'S ALL THAT remained between Michigan State and a national championship. Easier said than done, however. All of the top teams in the country have the same idea, while the lesser teams that receive bids to the NCAA Tournament dream of becoming a Cinderella story. In other words, everyone wants to win it more than they've ever wanted anything in sports. For college basketball teams, to be part of the Final Four and emerge the winner is the absolute ultimate.

The Spartans were entering the tournament on a roll. They had started the season with a 9–1 run and closed it by going 10–1 over the final eleven games. Maybe they needed that 2–4 slump in between. It not only brought them closer together as a team but also showed them the style of ball playing they *had* to play to achieve their greatest degree of success. It was going to be run, run, run throughout the NCAA tournament. And the man quarterbacking the show: Magic Johnson. By this time all of the Spartans knew what he meant to the team.

"We needed the things he brought here starting last year," said Greg Kelser. "I don't think it took any adjustment because he was the new guy. He was so far advanced than any freshman in the country. We understood this and we needed it."

Terry Donnelly saw it as much a matter of personality as basketball skills. "[Earvin] has a personality that's like Muhammad Ali's," said the Spartan guard. "It's classy, not conceited or anything. There have been times when he was actually running down the floor telling jokes. He's always smiling, always laughing. Never a frown on his face. Everyone likes a guy like that."

For Coach Heathcote the pass was the thing, always the pass. "When you can make a pass that leads to a basket," he explained, "where the receiver has nothing to do other than put it in the hoop, the pass is more important than the basket. Earvin has proved that."

Magic was drawing raves, all right. He was again a consensus All-American with the speculation that an NBA career was just around the corner. It would seem that he was, by far, college basketball's most exciting player and the one man all eyes would be upon during the NCAA tourney. But that wasn't the case. There was another player who had been competing all year with Magic for headlines. He was the same guy who had combined with Magic for those spectacular, no-look passes during the all-star team tour the summer before. Larry Bird of Indiana State was a whole separate story in himself.

Bird was a 6'9" forward who had made a conscious decision to play his college ball at Indiana State

University, certainly not a mecca of big-time basketball. Born in the tiny town of French Lick, Indiana, Bird was nearly three years older than Magic but had become equally impassioned by the sport. He was fortunate to have excellent coaches in high school who taught him the way the game was supposed to be played. No short-cuts. Just fundamental basketball. Bird's talent and cre-ativity took over from there.

Because he was so good and from a state that had always considered basketball an activity to be nurtured and in some cases nearly worshiped, he was pressured to pursue a big time college career. That meant the University of Indiana, which was a perennial court pow-erhouse under taskmaster coach Bobby Knight. Larry was intensely recruited by Knight and finally agreed to go there in the fall of 1974.

It was a bad mix. A small-town kid, Bird wasn't ready for a 30,000-student campus. He was totally unhappy there and stayed for just a month. "The school was too big and I couldn't get adjusted," he would say.

He next tried a two-year junior college but didn't remain there, either. So it was back home, where he got a job with the French Lick Department of Sanitation. It all could have ended right then and there, especially when he also had to deal with the trauma of his father's death. Fortunately for Larry and the basket-ball world, the people at Indiana State didn't give up.

The state-run university was only about a third of the size of Indiana with a lot less pressure. It still took a trip to French Lick by then assistant coach Bill Hodges to get Larry to consider trying again. Hodges found Larry coming out of a Laundromat with his grandmother. He followed them to her house and talked to Larry about the Indiana State program. In the fall of 1975 Larry Bird decided to give college one more try.

This time it worked out. Larry had to redshirt his

first year because he was considered a transfer, but the next year he joined the team and single-handedly turned the team and the program into something special. The Sycamores played in the Missouri Valley Conference and were far from a national power. But the team finished 25–3 Larry's first year, as he averaged nearly 33 points and 13 rebounds a game.

Bird was a deceptive ballplayer. He didn't look very fast and couldn't jump high, but his skills and his feeling for the game were so great that his lack of speed and jumping ability weren't handicaps at all. His jump shot was classic in form and his range unlimited. Yet he could also go to the hoop and work in close with either hand. Like Magic, he had an uncanny sixth sense when it came to knowing his teammates' whereabouts on the court and his passes were things to behold. His timing and ability to box out were so highly developed that he could rebound successfully against bigger men and better leapers. In a nutshell, there was nothing Larry Bird couldn't do. His skills, drive, and determination made the players around him better. His presence enabled them to raise the level of their games by a notch or two. Sound familiar?

During his junior year in 1977–78, as Magic Johnson was leading Michigan State into the top ten, Larry Bird was doing the same for Indiana State. The Sycamores were beginning to defeat better teams and were becoming a threat to everyone. They finished the season at 23–9, with Bird averaging 30 points a game and impressing everyone.

In fact, Larry could have declared hardship and gone to the NBA right then and there. He already knew where he would be going. The cagey Red Auerbach, general manager of the Boston Celtics, saw greatness in the blond-haired kid from French Lick and drafted him that year as a "future." That meant if Bird didn't come out, the Celtics would still have a chance to sign him the following year.

Because he felt an obligation to Indiana State, Larry decided to remain for his senior year. It was a good choice because it set the scene for one of college basketball's classic confrontations. Bird was absolutely brilliant all year. His supporting cast just wasn't that good, but Larry Bird refused to let them lose. By the time the NCAA tournament rolled around, Indiana State was undefeated and the number one ranked team in the country.

Critics talked about a soft schedule. The Sycamores played only a few of the top twenty teams. But no matter who the opponent, Larry Bird was the dominant player on the floor. About the only other quality player on the team was guard Carl Nicks. So in the eyes of many, Indiana State was about as close to a one-man team as it could possibly be.

In a sense that rap detracted from Bird's performance. Because he was the main man, Larry had to carry the load. But in reality he was a consummate team player who, like Magic Johnson, would do whatever it took to win. At the outset of the NCAA tournament there were already a number of people looking over the draw in anticipation. Should both Michigan and Indiana State keep winning, the two teams wouldn't meet until the championship game.

Michigan State seemed to have an easy matchup in the first round. Magic and company would have to meet tiny Lamar, which had upset the University of Detroit. Though the Spartans were heavy favorites, they couldn't afford to take any game lightly. A number of highly ranked teams have fallen victim to early-round upsets in the championships. If a hungry Cinderella school catches a giant napping, it can easily sneak past him.

This wasn't the case in the Michigan State–Lamar game. Magic had the Spartans running and they rolled to a 95–64 victory. But it turned out to be a costly one. Center Jay Vincent came out of the game with a stress fracture in his foot. His playing time would be severely limited for the remainder of the tournament. The injury had everyone worried. As Magic admitted, "We weren't long on depth."

But injuries notwithstanding, a team has to go on. In the regional semifinals the Spartans were scheduled to meet Louisiana State. Like all of the other coaches who had faced Magic and the Spartans, LSU's Dale Brown tried to come up with a plan to slow down the Michigan State express. He was hoping his team could take an early lead and then control the pace, just freeze the ball during the rest of the game.

The strategy didn't work. Greg Kelser intercepted a pair of LSU passes in the opening minutes. Each time he raced down court, flew through the air, and dunked with a flourish. So it was the Spartans who grabbed the early lead and from there they were never headed. Magic then took control and led the way with 24 points and 12 assists in an 87–71 win.

One thing the Spartans had been doing a bit differently down the stretch was to allow Magic to swing back and forth from guard to forward. When he went up front, Mike Brkovich would move into the backcourt. In certain situations they would flipflop the other way. Magic still did the bulk of the ball-handling, but the slight change in strategy gave the offense another dimension.

"I had thought that Earvin could just destroy people at guard," Coach Heathcote said, "but I learned he needs the freedom of being able to set up inside and outside both."

It was a subtle change, but it was working. Now the Spartans were in the regional finals against a good Notre Dame team. The winner would be headed to Salt Lake City and the Final Four. But this one wasn't easy. The Irish were a deep team and Coach Digger Phelps rotated nine players during the course of the game, prompting Coach Heathcote to remark: "Notre Dame goes at you with nine players, and we come back at you with two."

He was referring, of course, to the combination of Johnson and Kelser. Though he didn't mean to slight his other starters, it was a strange thing for a coach to say, albeit not far from the truth. The players were ready. Magic even remarked that the Spartans wanted Notre Dame and Digger Phelps "so badly we could taste it."

Notre Dame's plans were to put 6'7" guard Bill Hanzlik on Magic. Hanzlik had the reputation of being a tenacious defender. But when he heard about the Irish's plan Greg Kelser just laughed.

"If it were me," he said, "I'd say something about his mother and then hope he'd hit me and get thrown out of the game."

As for Magic, he was making sounds like it was now or never for the Spartans, that this was the year they had to win it.

"I don't think State will be back next year," he told a reporter. "Kelser is a senior and, as for me, I don't know what I'm going to do about the pros. So this is it. This is our chance right here."

It was yet another indication that Magic was already thinking NBA. Maybe he was only trying to motivate his teammates. Either way, the Spartans were ready. They showed it with the opening tap.

Kelser jumped center and tapped the ball straight to Magic. Without looking, Magic flipped the ball over his head to Brkovich, who was already streaking to the basket. The set play resulted in a quick dunk and the fans went wild. Magic and Brkovich high-fived and the tone was set. Once again the Spartans ran the Irish dizzy and never allowed them back into the game. They won it easily, 80–68, and were headed to the Final Four. Kelser wound up with a game high of 34 points, while Magic handed out 13 assists.

"That's our offense," Terry Donnelly joked. "One passes and the other one dunks."

It wasn't their only offense, but sometimes it seemed that way. Once again fans and coaches marveled at the overall court sense and passing ability of Magic Johnson. At each and every game he seemed to do something new, something different. Terry Donnelly said again that this was a quality Magic had shown to his teammates from day one.

"I had heard the stories even before Magic arrived on campus," Donnelly said. "But it didn't really hit me until I got in the backcourt with him the first day of practice. You're running down the floor and you're open. Most people can't get the ball to you through two or three people, but with Magic all of a sudden the ball is in your hands and you've got a lay-up."

After their victory in the Mideast final, which had been held in Indianapolis, the Spartans returned to East Lansing. But Coach Heathcote decided to take his club to Salt Lake City early. They flew out on Wednesday even though the semifinals weren't scheduled until Saturday. The coach apparently sensed a cocky mood on campus, a feeling that the national championship was in the bag. He didn't want a false sense of confidence permeating his team. A few good practices out there and the confidence would be genuine.

Getting there two days early proved a pleasant experience. The entire team was invited to a chalet at a ski resort outside of Salt Lake City. It seems there was a Spartan fan out there who owned the resort and the team was able to relax on Thursday, enjoying the magnificent views of the mountains.

Then the other teams arrived. One was powerful DePaul, the number-two team in the country. The Blue Demons were the sentimental favorite because of their longtime coach, Ray Meyer. Meyer had been at DePaul since the early 1940s, when he helped George Mikan develop into basketball's first great big man. But Meyer had never won a national title and hadn't been to the Final Four in thirty-six years.

The Cinderella team was the University of Pennsylvania, an Ivy League entry that had surprised everyone by winning the Eastern Regional. The Quakers would be facing Magic Johnson and Michigan State in one semifinal. Facing DePaul in the other semi was none other than Larry Bird and Indiana State.

To the astonishment of some so-called experts, the Sycamores had met and passed every test on the road to Salt Lake City. Maybe they had a soft schedule and maybe they shouldn't have been ranked number one, but Larry Bird had now proved to all that he was a player of superb ability. Bird was on a roll and he was bringing his Indiana State teammates with him.

He was also doing it with a triple fracture of the left thumb, an injury sustained against New Mexico State in the final game of the Missouri Valley Conference Tournament. The Sycamores won it, 69–59, to get an automatic bid to the NCAAs, but the injury to Bird left the team in limbo. If their great star couldn't play, the rest of the team might as well play in their street clothes. That's how long they would be around.

The alternatives for Bird were to sit out or at best play with the thumb in some kind of cumbersome splint or even a cast. He chose neither. He would continue to play with the thumb simply bandaged.

"I've been in sports eighteen years," said Indiana State trainer Bob Behnke, "and Larry is the toughest athlete I've seen. A lot of guys would have been sitting and watching after that kind of injury. Not Larry. He didn't give sitting a second thought and didn't complain once. And, believe me, that thumb hurt."

Pain or no, Bird tossed in 22 points in a victory over Virginia Tech, then lit it up for 29 as the Sycamores defeated a tough Oklahoma team. In the regional final Indiana State had to play Arkansas, a powerhouse team featuring All-American Sidney Moncrief. It turned out to be an outstanding basketball game.

Before the game, Arkansas coach Eddie Sutton was asked about containing Bird. His answer was interesting, because he could just as easily have been talking about another Final Four All-American.

"You're not going to stop him," said Sutton of Bird, "but you can slow him down. He hurts you most with his passing; in fact, he's the best passer for a big man I've ever seen. We've got to try to take the pass away from him."

Sutton was also describing Magic Johnson to a tee. He and Bird both played the complete game and often hurt opponents more with their passing than their scoring. That's why many basketball purists were hoping the two great stars would meet in the final.

The Indiana State–Arkansas game was exciting from start to finish. For the entire first half and for the first seven minutes of the second half, Bird dominated. He had 25 points in the first twenty-seven minutes of action, but the game remained close, the Sycamores holding a small lead. Then Coach Sutton gambled and put the 6'5" Moncrief on Bird. Using his quickness and defensive tenacity, the All-American Moncrief did an outstanding job of denying Bird the ball.

He didn't stop Bird completely, but with two minutes left the score was tied at 71–all and Arkansas had the ball. By that time Larry had tallied 31 points and the Razorbacks didn't want to give him the chance to win it. They decided to hold for the last shot. But with 1:08 left Arkansas turned it over. Now Indiana State would have a shot at the victory.

Naturally the Sycamores wanted the ball in Bird's hands. He finally got it with just eleven seconds left, but Moncrief was all over him, playing brilliant defense. Too smart to force a shot, Bird managed to pass the ball to Steve Reed, who went up to take a jumper from the top of the key. But while in the air he dumped the ball off to sub forward Bob Heaton on the left baseline. Heaton threw up a last-second shot with his left hand. It hit the rim, bounced high in the air . . . and fell through. The Sycamores had won it, 73–71, and were on their way to the Final Four. In the eyes of many, this still-unbeaten ballclub was a team of destiny. Bird was both their star and their good-luck charm. Maybe they thought they would surprise all the experts and win it all. But first they would have to get past DePaul.

So the cast of characters was finally gathered. Most of the reporters and media people wanted to talk with either Magic or Bird. Though their on-court games were similarly brilliant, the two superstars were decidedly different away from the hardwood. Magic was gregarious, outgoing, with a friendly word and a quick smile for everyone. He was what was termed a good interview, a youngster who was engaging if not profound.

Larry Bird, on the other hand, was shy and withdrawn, slightly suspicious, almost taciturn in his approach to the media. He might not have been a good interview, but that didn't mean he wasn't a good guy. He just wasn't used to the attention. Earvin Johnson was, having already been in the spotlight for years. After all, he was the Magic man, the kid with the perfect nickname. Bird didn't even have a nickname. He simply went out and played the game.

"I'm lovin' all of this," Magic proclaimed. "Every minute of it. It's exciting. I'm really having a good time. In fact, I'm having a ball. I feel like a kid going to a birthday party. Being in the Final Four, getting all the attention, having your name in all the newspapers in the country. You gotta love it."

Magic never lost his smile, despite being asked repeatedly to compare himself with Bird and about whether he would turn pro. He felt it was unfair to compare his personality with Bird's. After all, they were two distinctly different individuals. As for turning pro, well . . .

"How can I think about that when I have a chance for the national championship?" he asked. "That's what everyone's been asking me. Pro, pro, pro, pro. What about pro? We'll see after Monday night. Maybe."

For Michigan State the Saturday semifinal was no sweat. Penn was simply overmatched and they seemed to be suffering a bad case of stage fright. The Spartans ran their Ivy League opponents out of the game within minutes of the opening tap. It seemed as if every time Greg Kelser went to the hoop Magic had the ball waiting for him. It was a thing of beauty.

"A little eye contact is all we need," Kelser would say. "I know what [Magic] is looking for, and he knows what I'm looking for."

The Spartans continued to fast break. At one point the score was an embarrassing 38–8. By halftime it was 50–17, the widest first-half margin in Final Four history. From there Michigan State simply coasted home with a 101–67 victory. In forty-eight hours they would be playing for the national championship.

Once again it was the Johnson and Kelser show.

Magic had 29 points, 10 rebounds, and 10 assists, a future triple double. Kelser was right behind him with 28 points and 9 caroms. They truly made it look easy.

The only one who made it look easy in the second semifinal was Larry Bird. Once again this outstanding ballplayer came through in the clutch. To the casual observer he played an almost perfect game. Those who knew him better said the broken thumb seemed to hamper his rebounding and ball-handling. Fortunately, nothing bothered his shooting—not the thumb, not the DePaul defense, not the capacity crowd.

Indiana State needed Bird's deadly shooting because DePaul, led by freshman Mark Aguirre, was also playing a strong game. During the first half the score was tied on fifteen separate occasions with neither team managing more than a 4-point lead. Then with Bird leading the way, the Sycamores came out of the gate fast at the beginning of the second half. After a little more than three minutes had passed, they had spurted to an 11-point lead and it looked as if they were taking control of the game.

But then the tide of the game seemed to turn. Maybe it was Bird's thumb. The trainer had said the pain was intense and it had to become worse as the game, with all its banging and bumping, wore on. Larry was committing more turnovers and his ball-handling seemed a bit tentative. It let DePaul back into the game.

From a 67–61 deficit the Blue Demons hit six straight shots. Indiana State had just a pair of hoops during that time, giving DePaul the lead for the first time at 73–71. There was just 4:59 left. At this point DePaul began holding the ball. Meyer ordered a version of the North Carolina four-corner offense, a spread formation designed to slow things to a crawl. But the strategy backfired when the Blue Demons committed a turnover. Bird whipped a quick pass to Bob Heaton, who hit a lay-up to tie the game with just 3:27 left.

DePaul reclaimed the lead with 1:37 remaining when guard Gary Garland hit a free throw. But he missed the second and Bird grabbed the rebound. Some forty-seven seconds later Carl Nicks drove down the middle and dumped a pass off to Heaton, who hit yet another lay-up. Now the Sycamores were up one, 75–74. DePaul had one more shot at it, but Mark Aguirre's twenty-foot jumper with four seconds left bounced off the rim and into the hands of Indiana State's Leroy Staley. Staley was fouled and his one free throw made the final score 76–74. Indiana State had done it and the Bird-Johnson matchup was a reality.

As usual, Bird had led the way with a sterling 16-for-19 shooting performance, good for 35 points. He also had a game-high 16 rebounds and added 9 assists. The only negative was his surprising 11 turnovers.

"If I had known I would make eleven turnovers I would have thought we would lose," Larry said afterward. "We were very lucky."

Now it seemed that everyone was concentrating on the big Monday matchup. Magic versus Bird. Both superstars wanted the emphasis on their respective teams, but it doesn't work that way. It's the big guys who attract the attention and get most of the ink. Magic experienced that situation at both Everett High and Michigan State. Even some of the other players were asked about the first meeting ever between Johnson and Bird.

"I'd like to go out and watch it myself," said Terry Donnelly. "You can't help getting caught up in a confrontation like this."

Coach Heathcote also knew the biggest challenge his team would face was corraling Bird, who wore the same uniform number 33 as his magic counterpart.

"From what I've seen of Bird," Heathcote quipped,

"he's not just one bird. He's a whole flock!"

But the coach also had a scheme to control the flock and keep it from flying too high. It was a kind of matchup zone that would, in Heathcote's words, put "a man and a half on Bird" at all times. When Bird had the ball, the Spartans would try to clog up as many of the passing lanes as they could. The team had plenty of practice doing this when they defended Magic at their own practice sessions.

With more than 15,000 screaming fans anticipating every move by the two superstars, the game got underway. The Spartans wanted to run early, discourage the Sycamores, and try to blow them out of the building. It didn't happen immediately, but less than five minutes into the game Terry Donnelly hit a jump shot to put Michigan State into the lead. And once they were in front, the Spartans were very difficult to catch.

To make matters worse, Indiana State wasn't looking sharp. They couldn't seem to find a cohesiveness, a rhythm. Part of the reason was the matchup zone. Bird was being harassed every time he got the ball and was having difficulty finding open teammates. Part of it might have been the painful thumb injury; the other part was the Spartan dominance.

As usual, Magic and Kelser were doing the job, fast-breaking whenever the opportunity arose and outrunning the Sycamores, as they had been outrunning everyone else during the past month and a half. By halftime Michigan State had a 37–28 lead and the players could sense the title. Then, early in the second half, the Spartans got a lift from an unlikely source.

Early in the session Terry Donnelly had hit a jumper. The Spartans came downcourt again and Magic got the ball to Donnelly. Boom. He buried a second jumper. Twice more in a short span Donnelly canned jumpers as Magic kept feeding the hot man. His four straight baskets opened up a 16-point lead for Michigan State. That just about did it right then and there.

Bird and his teammates wouldn't quit. They fought back and at one point cut the lead back to six. But they could come no closer. With the score at 61–54, Indiana State had the ball four consecutive times and didn't score once. Plus they were blowing free throws throughout the game, as the aggressive Spartan defense committed a high number of fouls.

From there Michigan State coasted home, winning the game, 75–64, and the national championship. When it ended, Magic had 24 points and 7 rebounds, while Kelser canned 19 and grabbed 8 boards. Terry Donnelly, a 6.3 per game scorer to that point, surprised everyone with 15. As for Larry Bird, he had had a frustrating night, hitting just 7 of 21 field-goal tries and finishing with 19 points. He led everyone with 13 rebounds, but it wasn't enough. Still, he had taken his team through thirty-three straight victories. There was nothing to be ashamed of, but with competitors like Magic and Larry every loss hurts, no matter how big or how small.

"Larry was very, very frustrated throughout the game," said Jay Vincent, who played sparingly because of his foot injury. "He kept saying 'Give me the ball,' but his teammates couldn't get it to him."

Shortly before the game ended, Magic and Greg Kelser embraced at midcourt. In a sense it was almost like a good-bye. Afterward, Kelser spoke for everyone when he said: "We'd been a very, very good team the last month. I felt that if we won we could say we are a great team. Well, we are. We play together and we use the talent that we have."

While Larry Bird retreated to lick his wounds and begin to think about his future with the Boston Celtics, Magic Johnson spent a quiet but happy evening with his parents, and his teammates and their parents. Then everyone returned to East Lansing for a huge pep rally at Jenison Field House. It was among the best of times. Coach Heathcote and all of the players took turns talking to the enthusiastic crowd. When Magic rose to speak, a spontaneous chant began, building in volume and emotion.

TWO MORE YEARS! TWO MORE YEARS! TWO MORE YEARS!

Everyone, including Magic, knew what it meant. The fans wanted their popular star to return and complete his college career. Magic smiled and waved. Then he said: "We had a mission to accomplish and we did it!"

TWO MORE YEARS! TWO MORE YEARS! TWO MORE YEARS!

More smiles, maybe a bit nervous now. He had just been part of a national championship team, had been the most valuable player of the final game and was celebrating. Yet the pressure of another big decision already loomed in front of him. It was so direct he felt compelled to address it.

"I don't know now about two more years," he said. "I don't know what I will do. But whatever it is, I hope you continue to support me."

It would be a difficult and important decision, all right. But somewhere deep down inside his subconscious, Earvin Johnson already knew what had to be done.

CHAPTER

FIVE

NBA Rookie, Circa 1979

AS A COLLEGIAN, IT SEEMED THAT MAGIC Johnson had no more worlds to conquer. Almost, that is. His stats as a sophomore were remarkably consistent with those of his freshman year. He averaged 17.1 points a game, had 234 rebounds and 269 assists. His shooting percentage was just 46.8, a weakness some said, though Magic always insisted, "I can shoot."

He was again a consensus All-American and had now played with a national champion. The one prize that eluded him was the coveted Player of the Year Award. That went to—you guessed it—Larry Bird. It would be hard to argue the choice. But in the eyes of many, all Magic had to do was stay around for another year and the prize would be his. Would that be motivation enough to return? Magic, of course, had the option of those two more years. Around East Lansing and indeed in many other places, the would-he-or-wouldn't-he decision to be made by Magic Johnson was the prime topic of conversation. Everyone had an opinion but only one man knew the answer.

Logic dictated that Magic would turn pro. After all, he was at the zenith of the college game. It was already acknowledged that his physical skills and strength were of professional caliber. No secret there. If he stayed another year, even two, his value to an NBA team would probably not go appreciably higher. The reason was simple. It already was sky high.

In addition, with Greg Kelser leaving the team, there was little likelihood of the Spartans repeating their NCAA run, even with Magic's presence. Sure, if he stayed he would probably become player of the year. But finishing second to Larry Bird was no disgrace and to stay just to win a single award wasn't a very solid reason.

Of course, there was also the academic part of it. Magic had always maintained a very good grade point level. That was important to him. But he never hid the fact that academics were secondary to basketball. His dream was to play in the NBA, and as he had already said, a player coming out early could always go back and finish his degree. These were all reasons pointing toward his coming out.

The injury factor also had to be considered. Magic's high market value could disappear the same instant that a ligament in his knee was torn. Don't laugh. It could happen and was certainly, at this point, something to consider. Of course, there were those who wanted Magic to return to State, namely those people who would benefit the most: his coach, his teammates, and the entire Michigan State populace.

"College basketball is fun," said old friend Jay

Vincent. "What's better than that? I don't think [Earvin] should go pro and I don't think he will."

Coach Heathcote voiced a similar sentiment. "I want what's best for Earvin," he said, "and what's best for him is to stay. I could give you a lot of reasons. But then again, there's the specter of a couple of million dollars . . ."

One of his professors felt Magic should finish his four years because "it would be a stylish way to go." And cries of "Two more years!" were reverberating outside his dorm window day and night. In a sense it was a battle between the philosophical and the practical, between the world of academia and the world of business. But then again the world of college athletics was rapidly becoming as big a business as anything else. Before Magic went to Michigan State, for example, ticket sales during the basketball season produced revenue of $150,000. Three years later that figure had jumped to some $425,000. In addition, winning the NCAA championship could be worth literally millions to a university. So how could anyone castigate Earvin Johnson if he considered the dollars that could come his way as a pro?

In fact, for Magic it was a combination of dollars and a dream. And that's tough to beat, especially when something else was added to the mix that was beginning to bubble with expectation. That something else was the fun factor.

"One thing I'm always going to have is fun," Magic said. "There is a time for business, a time for school and a time for fun. I love life and I'm getting so much enjoyment out of it. That's what I want for others, too. When a guy pays $3 or $4 for a ticket, I want him to get a show from me. And he will because I always have to please myself, and I always manage to do that."

Magic also felt that Larry Bird would be the number-one man coming into the NBA in 1979–80. There was, however, no chance of Bird being the number-one draft choice. He was already spoken for because Boston's wily Red Auerbach had had the foresight to pick him as a future. But Bird was obviously still on Magic's mind, maybe as a measuring stick.

"I don't think I'm worth as much as Bird," he said. "Larry has played longer and has got experience. Besides, he's a white superstar and basketball needs him. But think of me in the NBA, too."

Magic's three main advisors were thinking about it and among them there was a 2–1 split. His mother felt he should stay in school and get his degree. Her theory was he could always play pro ball. But both his father and Charles Tucker felt he was ready and the time was right. His market value was at an all-time high and now the risk of injury was definitely a factor. The three men also agreed that Magic had accomplished nearly everything he could creatively as a collegian.

One other friend, more removed from the situation than the others, also felt it was time for the NBA. George Fox, who had coached Magic at Everett, put it this way: "You cannot, in good conscience, advise him to turn down millions. Anyone who does is selfish and is not looking out for Earvin's best interests."

There was still another consideration. It was generally acknowledged that if he opted for the pros, Magic would be the league's number-one choice. So there had to be some concern about which team had the choice. A year earlier it was the Kansas City Kings. The Kings were not a strong team and, at the time, were based in the Midwest. Though Magic and his advisors did meet with the Kings, there was probably no real strong desire on his part to play with them. It would have taken a contract of huge proportions to convince him.

The team with the top choice can also trade that choice right up to draft day, so there is no certainty

which team would pick first until almost the last minute.
In 1979 there would be a coin flip to determine which
club had number one. It was between the Chicago Bulls
and the Los Angeles Lakers. Both teams were in major
media markets and would have a great deal to offer a
marketable commodity like Magic. With his warm personality and great smile, he would be an ideal
spokesman for a variety of products and/or companies.
So his endorsement potential was also very great.

The Bulls, however, were not a very good basketball
team. They were a club that needed rebuilding badly,
and what better player to serve as a cornerstone than
Magic Johnson? The Bulls were in the running for the
top draft choice because of their position in the stand-
ings. The Lakers, on the other hand, were a winning
team, a ballclub anchored by the great 7'1" center
Kareem Abdul-Jabbar. Definitely not one of the league's
have-nots, L.A. was in the running for the top draft
choice by virtue of a trade made three years earlier.

In 1976 the Lakers had lost high-scoring guard Gail
Goodrich to free agency. When Goodrich signed with
the then New Orleans Jazz, the Jazz were required to
give the Lakers compensations. It was in the form of
several draft choices, one of which was New Orleans'
top pick in 1979. Now that top pick meant a shot at
number one. Both the Lakers and the Bulls indicated
that the two top players on their lists were Earvin
Johnson and Sidney Moncrief of Arkansas.

While he was awaiting the coin flip to determine
which team would go first, Magic continued to vacillate.
Friends said that one day it was yes, the next no. He
thoroughly enjoyed campus life and everything else
associated with Michigan State. But the lure of the pro
game was also strong. Finally Magic himself admitted
that his decision would hinge on the team and on the
size of the contract they were willing to give him.

The coin toss was held on April 19, 1979. Commissioner Larry O'Brien flipped the coin and when it landed it came up Lakers. Now Magic would have three weeks to decide whether to declare hardship or not. He knew the Bulls wanted him very badly, but he couldn't be sure about the Lakers. Los Angeles already had an outstanding young point guard in Norm Nixon. Maybe they would opt to fill a particular need rather than choose the most exciting player.

NCAA rules allowed an underclassman who was thinking of declaring hardship to use a lawyer to help negotiate and interpret possible contract clauses. Magic knew that the one thing he had going for him was the option of not coming out, of returning to school. He and his advisors felt that a deal had to be made before the deadline to declare hardship.

Magic and his family (including Charles Tucker) finally chose a law firm in Chicago. He would be represented by George and Harold Andrews, who came highly recommended by Gus Ganakas, who had been the Michigan State coach before Jud Heathcote. Both attorneys felt that besides negotiating a contract, they should also devise a total financial plan for their client. Even then Magic wanted not only to be part of everything in which he was involved, he wanted to be in control of it. Too many athletes have left their money completely in the hands of others and, as a result, suffered financially for it. Magic's lawyers felt it should be that way and all parties agreed.

Shortly afterward, Laker owner Jack Kent Cooke sent word that Magic would be his team's first choice . . . if an agreement could be worked out. For a while the two sides played the negotiating game. It was like a pair of fighters during the first round. Nobody wanted to commit. They just felt each other out with light jabs and fancy footwork, hoping to spot a weakness, get a feeling of who wanted whom more.

Basketball salaries in 1979 had not yet escalated into the multimillion-dollar stratosphere, but the numbers were getting higher. The top Laker in terms of yearly dollars was Abdul-Jabbar, who was in the $650,000 range. Magic and his advisors knew they couldn't ask for more than that. For the time being Kareem had to be the highest-paid Laker. So they settled on an even $500,000 as the number they would seek.

The negotiations weren't easy. Jack Kent Cooke was a shrewd businessman, well versed in the negotiation process and the resultant psychological warfare between the negotiating parties. He wined and dined Earvin and his advisors in Los Angeles but still didn't make it easy for them to come to an agreement. At one point Cooke offered $400,000 as a base salary, and the Johnson camp countered with a $600,000 request.

That's when Cooke said, flat out, that the Lakers could win with or without Magic, reminding him that the team had been in the playoffs seventeen of the past nineteen years. It wasn't so different from two heads of state trying to negotiate a piece of disputed land or the return of prisoners of war. We don't need the land. We can live without it. But if you want to give it back, here's what we'll offer. Verbal fencing. It was something Jack Kent Cooke did in business every day and apparently enjoyed.

Earvin and his people had only the experience of the year before with the Kings, but they held their ground. But once Cooke gave them the we-can-win-with-or-without-you line, Magic felt he had had enough. He stood up and said he was going back to school. That's when the Laker owner stopped them and implored them to remain in Los Angeles for one more night. He promised them they wouldn't be disappointed.

The next morning the offer was up to $460,000. Again the two sides played tag. They were meeting at the Lakers' home, the Great Western Forum, and

Cooke showed Magic pictures of some past Laker greats: Jerry West, Elgin Baylor, Wilt Chamberlain. He added that Kareem was there now and that he very much wanted Magic to be part of the tradition. Seconds later he raised the offer to $500,000 and Magic stuck out his hand. It was settled. Earvin Johnson would be a Los Angeles Laker.

He returned to East Lansing. A press conference was called three days later and Magic told his friends, as well as the rest of the world, that he was going to forgo his final two years at Michigan State and become a professional. Five days after that he was back in Los Angeles for an even bigger press conference.

This one was hosted by longtime Laker broadcaster, the gravel-voiced Chick Hearn. The purpose was to introduce Magic to the L.A. media. Hearn opened the press conference by saying: "Ladies and gentlemen, this is one of the most historic events in Laker history." He went on to describe Magic as a "breath of fresh air who will breathe new life into the Los Angeles Lakers," and added that he didn't remember "a young man in recent years, maybe ever, who has captivated fans the way Magic has."

The only thing premature was that Magic wasn't officially a Laker yet. In accordance with NBA rules, that couldn't happen until the draft was held some six weeks later. Technically, they were just announcing that Magic and the Lakers had agreed to agree. But in reality the paperwork was already completed and had been signed. A month and a half later Commissioner Larry O'Brien made the formal announcement. Earvin "Magic" Johnson was the first choice of the Los Angeles Lakers, the first rookie picked in the 1979 NBA draft.

* * *

What kind of rookie would Earvin Johnson make? There have been, after all, number-one choices who turned out to be more turkey than terrific. During Magic's final year at Michigan State he was part of a scouting report that rated the pro potential of the top college players. Wherever there was a negative, or perhaps it's more accurate to say a less-than-glowing positive, there was a following statement to qualify the evaluation.

For example, the report said that "speed is not his greatest attribute." But it added that he had the quickness to make the initial offensive move to beat most defenders. And it described him as "very fast when he has the ball, especially on the break."

Where the report rated him as only "an average jumper for his size," it went on to say that he "rebounds extremely well for a guard" and that he "knows how to box out and has a nose for the ball."

When the report called his shooting the area that drew the most criticism, it also said that he "has the ability to become a competent shooter." It also suggested that fans "watch him when MSU needs two points." The report also qualified the evaluation by saying that he "thinks pass before a shot," and that many of the shots were last-resort decisions and taken off balance.

Magic wasn't called a great defensive player but an improving one, a guy "who has a nose for the ball and a knack for sizing up opponents and taking the ball away from them."

When it came to his ball-handling and passing, there were no negatives. He was rated tops in both categories. The report described Magic's uncanny court sense, saying that he knew where everyone was on the court almost all of the time. He was, the report said, "a remarkable passer on the fast break . . . few players see the passing lanes as well as Johnson."

In summing up Earvin Johnson the scouting report said that his "unselfish nature and enthusiasm for the game may be his greatest strengths. Given a chance, he'll find a way to beat you. And he has the poise and confidence to succeed."

That final statement might have been the key to Magic Johnson and one reason why the Lakers wanted him so badly. He was a winner who put life into a team, and while the Lakers were a winning ballclub, they were often viewed as a lifeless group of players who went through the motions. A victory didn't excite them any more than a loss upset them, or as one Los Angeles sportswriter put it, the Lakers "seem to win or lose with a shrug."

Even the fans at the Forum rarely showed any excessive emotion. Noise levels were low, almost as if they were watching a tennis match rather than a basketball game. But the entire league at the time had what Magic called a "cool" image. It wasn't cool to show emotion. Even Pat Williams, the general manager of the Philadelphia 76ers, commented on it.

"I think at least half of [Magic's] appeal is his enthusiasm," Williams said. "But you have to remember that happiness and glow and joy often turn to dust in our league."

Coming from a respected G.M., that was quite an indictment. Others made excuses for the all-too-often case of the blahs around the league, citing the long 82-game schedule, a sometimes grinding, tortuous affair that could wear down both body and mind. Magic was asked about keeping his college-type enthusiasm over a full season.

"It's impossible to play hard for 82 games," he said with a wink. "But I bet I can play hard in at least 70."

That remained to be seen. He didn't have to join the Lakers immediately after signing his contract. In fact, he was still in the process of finishing the semester at

Michigan State. Both Magic and Greg Kelser, who was a first-round pick of the Detroit Pistons, bought themselves new Mercedeses and tooled around the campus during the final weeks of school. It was an enjoyable, carefree time for both of them. They were pros, getting their first taste of play-for-pay luxury, yet they were still students and certainly big men on campus since the flames of a national championship still flared brightly in everyone's minds.

When Magic signed his contract with the Lakers, he became the highest-paid rookie in NBA history. That distinction didn't last long. Shortly afterward, Larry Bird signed with the Celtics for a first-year salary of approximately $600,000. Once again it was Bird and Johnson, now running 1–2 in the salary parade. They were 1–2 in the player of the year voting, and led their teams to a 1–2 finish in the NCAA Tournament. Now they were entering the NBA together and playing with teams that both had a long and successful history and a coast-to-coast rivalry that would once again heat up to incendiary proportions.

There was one other change before Magic reported to his first Laker training camp. Just a few weeks after Magic completed his personal contract negotiation with team owner Jack Kent Cooke, it was announced that Cooke had sold the team. The new owner was Jerry Buss, who had once earned a Ph.D. in chemistry and spent some time working in the aerospace industry. Dr. Buss decided, however, that he wanted something more. He went into the real estate business and became an American success story. He started with a $1,000 investment in a West Los Angeles apartment building and built it into a "multi-hundred-million-dollar real estate business at its height." After years of hard work, Dr. Buss decided to enjoy his money a little more and found himself the owner of an NBA team. In fact, at the same time he purchased the Lakers, he also bought the Los Angeles Kings of the National Hockey League, the Great Western Forum, and the 13,000-acre Kern County ranch. The price for all of this was $67.5 million in what was, at the time, the largest sports transaction in history.

Buss quickly became a hands-on owner who made it his business to know all of his players personally. He appeared in blue jeans and an open shirt as often as in a suit and a tie, and was not as distant as Jack Kent Cooke had been. Since he was a rookie owner the same year Earvin Johnson was a rookie player, the two hit it off immediately. In fact, when the two first met, it was a matter of enthusiastic owner meeting enthusiastic player, and it prompted the following exchange.

"I'm the happiest man in America," Dr. Buss said to Magic.

"No you're not," Magic answered quickly. "I am."

Both men laughed. They agreed they could be the two happiest men in America and took it from there. The question was, would the pressures and the egos involved in professional sports make one or both of them ultimately unhappy?

For the NBA to have two potentially super rookies coming into the league at the same time was welcome news. It didn't hurt that one of them—Larry Bird—was white in a league that had become dominated increasingly by black players, or that the second rookie— Magic Johnson— was a black man with a super personality to complement a super talent. The league needed a breath of fresh air and needed it badly.

Of the four so-called major sports—baseball, football, basketball, and hockey—basketball took the longest to organize into a stable professional league.

Baseball, of course, goes back before the turn of the century. The National Football League and the National Hockey League were both operating full-time by the 1920s. But basketball continued to have false starts and economic failures in its attempts to organize into a single professional league until the late 1940s.

The NBA as it is known today didn't begin play until the 1946–47 season. There were just eleven teams that first season, but three years later the league had expanded to seventeen franchises. Yet with the exception of a few so-called major market areas (New York, Boston, Philadelphia, Chicago), the league was mainly a small-town operation. There were franchises in Rochester, Fort Wayne, Anderson, Sheboygan, and Waterloo.

Then there was perhaps the strangest-named sports franchise ever, Tri-Cities. When the great Bob Cousy was first drafted, it was the Tri-Cities franchise that picked him. Cousy's first comment was "What's a Tri-Cities?" The franchise was so named because it had three home courts in three different cities, though the main base of operations was in Moline, Illinois.

No wonder, then, that the next few years saw franchises dropping out, folding, and moving. By 1951 there were ten teams and two years later just eight. But the league was finally beginning to stabilize.

In 1950 Red Auerbach and the Boston Celtics drafted a player from Duquesne, Chuck Cooper, the first black picked by an NBA team. Before the season was out, Cooper, Nat "Sweetwater" Clifton of the Knicks, and Earl Lloyd all broke the color line in the same year. Shortly afterward, the Minneapolis Lakers (the same franchise that would move to L.A.) became the league's first dominant team, winning five titles in six years with 6'10" George Mikan anchoring the ballclub from the center spot.

By the late 1950s the league was beginning to prosper. NBA games were on network television and more great stars were coming into the league. Bill Russell had joined the Boston Celtics in 1956–57, leading the team to the first of eleven championships in thirteen years, including an amazing eight in a row. Celtic domination might have been total, but at that time it was good for the popularity of the growing league. It gave pro basketball an identity.

In fact, the decade of the mid-1960s to the mid-1970s was almost a golden age for the NBA. Players were greater than ever and more new fans were discovering the court game as something to behold. Some of the earlier stars like Bob Cousy, Dolph Shayes, Paul Arizin, Bill Sharman, and Bob Pettit were already retired or winding down their careers. But the NBA roll in 1965, for instance, contained a slew of great and exciting players.

There were the big men, like Russell, Wilt Chamberlain, Nate Thurmond, Walt Bellamy, Zelmo Beaty, and Willis Reed. Some of the top forwards were Elgin Baylor, Jerry Lucas, Gus Johnson, Dave DeBusschere, Rick Barry, Bailey Howell, Chet Walter, Billy Cunningham, Bill Bridges, Lucious Jackson, Tom Sanders, and Rudy LaRusso.

And guards, wow, there were simply great playmakers, shooters and all-around stars everywhere. There was the Big O, Oscar Robertson, and the Lakers' Jerry West, still considered by many the two greatest ever. Then there were Guy Rodgers, K.C. and Sam Jones, Len Wilkens, Hal Greer, Richie Guerin, Dick Barnett, John Havlicek, Gail Goodrich, Walt Hazzard, and Jeff Mullins.

There were even more great players on the way. At that time, the NBA had a pretty even mix of black and white stars, and very little was said. But as the years rolled on, more and more black players began dominating the sport.

By 1975 many of the names had changed, but the league still had tremendous stars, players with individual identities and distinctive styles of play. Fans could enjoy the likes of Kareem Abdul-Jabbar, Bob McAdoo, "Pistol" Pete Maravich, Nate "Tiny" Archibald, "Downtown" Freddie Brown, George McGinnis, Calvin Murphy, Earl "The Pearl" Monroe, Walt "Clyde" Frazier, Elvin Hayes, Wes Unseld, Spencer Haywood, Bob Lanier, Dave Cowens, Paul Silas, "Slick" Watts, Dave Bing, Connie Hawkins, Jo Jo White, Bill Walton, and others. Basketball fans will always recognize these names in a flash. In addition, some of the veterans from the 1960s were still around.

But during this period a subtle change was taking place in the NBA and within four years there were definite problems. In 1976–77 there was a merger between the NBA and the young ABA. Four teams were absorbed and more exciting players like Julius Erving came into a league that now had twenty-two teams. The small-town franchises were long gone and the league was trying to concentrate on major market areas.

In 1978–79, however, twelve of the twenty-two teams reported that attendance was down from the previous year, a trend that had been continuing for several seasons. While Commissioner Larry O'Brien described the league as "stable," it was pointed out that the big four markets— New York, Los Angeles, Chicago, and Philadelphia—all saw drastic drops in attendance. Both the Knicks and the Bulls had woeful teams, and while the Lakers and the 76ers were still contenders they, too, weren't drawing.

Former Laker star Jerry West, now the team's coach, said quite emphatically, "People I talk to around Los Angeles tell me that there isn't a great deal of interest in either the Lakers or the NBA."

In addition, national TV ratings were down 26 percent, a huge loss. The first four Sunday telecasts of the year on CBS were trounced in the ratings by whatever events the other networks decided to run, including boxing, college basketball, and the *Superstars* a gimmicky, made-for-TV showcase in which well-known athletes competed against one another in sports other than their own. So there was growing concern about the future of the entire league.

Some felt the 82-game season was simply too long, that game and travel schedules wore down the players and made them complacent. More teams meant a longer playoff season and there was an increasing feeling that many players just went through the motions during the regular season, then turned it on during playoff time. It was also pointed out that the seven-game championship series between the Washington Bullets and the Seattle Supersonics in 1979 stretched out over eighteen days because of television commitments. And, as one writer said, "it was about as exciting as the pro bowlers' tour."

Another complaint was the scheduling of the increased number of teams. Each team played the other only four times a year, eliminating the old-fashioned traditional rivalries. In the 1960s, for example, fans could watch Bill Russell and Wilt Chamberlain go head-to-head some ten times a year. Same for Jerry West and Oscar Robertson. Or the Celtics and the Knicks, the Lakers and the Golden State Warriors. The schedule change was eliminating both team and individual rivalries. There would be, however, more conference games in 1979–80.

Ticket prices were also up all over the league, making it tougher for the average fan to afford too many games. And when those few games weren't very good and the players didn't seem to care, well, it doesn't take a genius to figure out what was happening.

Then there was the racial factor. Some people pretended it didn't exist. But by 1979 the stats showed that some 75 percent of the players were black, while 75 percent of the fans were white. More than one NBA executive said that the problem was becoming one of selling a predominantly black sport to a white public. Did working-class whites, for instance, who had trouble paying rising ticket prices resent black athletes who were making large sums of money?

Paul Silas of Seattle, an outstanding veteran player and president of the NBA Players' Association, felt there was a racial problem. He said that "people in general do not look favorably upon blacks who are making large sums of money if it appears they are not working hard for that money." Silas felt the players were so good that it appeared they were doing things too easily, that they didn't have the intensity they once had.

Others said they simply didn't have the intensity, at least not night after night. Here was Magic Johnson saying he could keep up the intensity for at least seventy games a year. A lot of players probably scoffed, saying wait till he gets here and tries it. But there was precedent. While the Celtics were dominating the league in the late 1950s and 1960s, the league already played an 80-game slate. Yet the Celtics had so much pride in their performance that, as a team, they would vow never to lose two games in a row. Of course, they did drop a pair once in a while. But they also won eleven championships in thirteen years. If that isn't long-term intensity, nothing is.

But intensity notwithstanding, the league did have image problems and was bent on correcting them. It decided to spend more money on promotion, quadruple its public relations budget, and hire an outside agency to work on image. Commissioner O'Brien also wanted to conduct a national survey to try to pinpoint the league's problems.

"I would be immensely disappointed and surprised if our survey showed race to be a problem," he said.

Though many felt the racial makeup of the league was a problem, they also felt that it could be alleviated by hardworking athletes. One general manager put it this way: "We look for good people. As far as our fan support goes, I honestly believe that if we had 10 black players and won, we would do just as well. When you're winning, fans forget skin color, salaries, everything. Winning solves all problems."

But there were winning teams where attendance was still down. Maybe the trick was winning with a flair and at the same time creating a feeling of a team, not of individuals. Seattle Coach Lenny Wilkens, himself a great former player, felt the team concept was still of paramount importance.

"This is still a team game," he said. "Unfortunately, we don't always show it that way. People want to see one guy score 30 points and make a great slam dunk. But that is not the game."

Now they were getting somewhere. Several other coaches like Jerry West and Golden State's Al Attles, both former players, one white and one black, agreed that the players coming into the league were bigger, stronger, faster, and quicker than those who had come before. But they were also dumber. They were not learning how the game should be played, rather they were relying on raw talent that would make them a lot of money and allow them to do things their way.

What to do? A public relations blitz? An improved image? A shorter schedule? More television exposure? Less television exposure? Everyone had an opinion. Paul Silas felt it was important to "make the fan understand that we are not sloughing off in our games." He felt if this could be done the public would change its perception of the players, realizing that most of them were hardworking and intelligent and cared about the sport and the communities. Then the black-white issue wouldn't matter.

Enter Earvin "Magic" Johnson and Larry Bird.

Facing the press as he announces his early retirement from the NBA after testing positive for the AIDS virus, Earvin "Magic" Johnson flashes his magnificent smile to millions of viewers around the world. *Photo credit: AP/Wide World Photos*

NCAA Basketball Championship players Magic Johnson of Michigan State and Larry Bird of Indiana State meet prior to the 1979 championship game. *Photo credit: AP/Wide World Photos*

"Who me?" Michigan State's Magic Johnson disputes a ref's call during the 1979 championship game against Indiana State. *Photo credit: AP/Wide World Photos*

Reaching high, Magic goes for a layup during the 1979 NCAA Championship Game between Michigan State and Indiana State. *Photo credit: AP/Wide World Photos*

A huge crowd of Lansing, Michigan, fans come out to greet the return of the 1979 NCAA Tournament's Most Valuable Player, Magic Johnson. *Photo credit: AP/Wide World Photos*

Magic heads to the L.A. Lakers and flashes his trademark smile at the news of being the first pick in the 1979 NBA draft. *Photo credit: AP/Wide World Photos*

Together with his parents, Mr. and Mrs. Earvin Johnson, Magic celebrates his first round draft pick by the Los Angeles Lakers. *Photo credit: AP/Wide World Photos*

Their first time playing against each other in the pros, Magic Johnson of the Lakers rips a rebound from the hands of Boston Celtics' Larry Bird. *Photo credit: AP/Wide World Photos*

With open arms, Magic thanks the L.A. Lakers' fans for the standing ovation they gave him on his first night back in uniform after knee surgery. *Photo credit: AP/Wide World Photos*

L.A. Lakers' Magic Johnson and Kareem Abdul-Jabbar share their joy after defeating the Boston Celtics for the 1985 NBA Championship title. *Photo credit: AP/Wide World Photos*

The smile of a champion. Magic accepts the NBA's Most Valuable Player award for the 1986-1987 season. *Photo credit: AP/Wide World Photos*

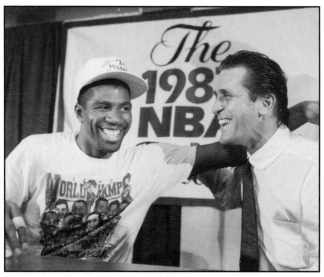

"Only the best." Los Angeles Lakers coach Pat Riley and guard Magic Johnson share a special moment after winning the 1987 NBA championship. *Photo credit: AP/Wide World Photos*

Clowning around during the 1987 NBA All Star Game are Los Angeles Lakers' Magic Johnson and Detroit's Isiah Thomas. *Photo credit: AP/Wide World Photos*

Magic, the video star. Magic relaxes during the taping of the 1986 "Choose Your Weapon" video in which he co-starred with Boston Celtics' Larry Bird. *Photo credit: AP/Wide World Photos*

L.A. Lakers' Magic Johnson finds the game of softball much more challenging than hoops after he swings and misses during a pickup game in 1981. *Photo credit: AP/Wide World Photos*

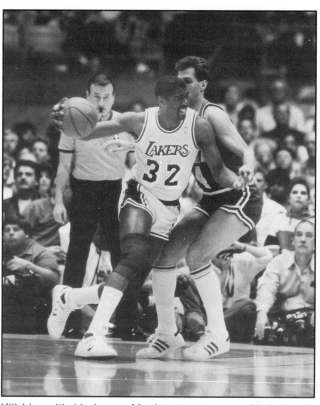

Kill him with kindness. Magic outmaneuvers Utah Jazz's Kelly Tripucka during a 1988 NBA game against the Lakers.
Photo credit: AP/Wide World Photos

Leaping detour. Lakers' guard Magic Johnson finds the only route to the hoop between Kansas City Kings' LaSalle Thompson and Don Buse during a 1984 NBA game. *Photo credit: AP/Wide World Photos*

The thrill of victory. Magic reacts after being presented with his championship ring for the 1987-88 season. *Photo credit: AP/Wide World Photos*

At his first appearance at the Forum since announcing his retirement, Magic shares a moment with Atlanta Hawks' Dominique Wilkins before the start of the Lakers game. *Photo credit: AP/Wide World Photos*

With his trademark smile and confidence, Magic waves to the fans at the L.A. Lakers–Atlanta Hawks game. His first appearance at a Laker game since his retirement, Magic was honored by fans with a standing ovation. *Photo credit: AP/Wide World Photos*

Not long after the start of the Lakers–Hawks game, Magic is on his feet yelling at referees from the sidelines. *Photo credit: AP/Wide World Photos*

The sign says it all. Young fans show their support and love for the man we know as Magic at a football game between the L.A. Rams and the Kansas City Chiefs. *Photo credit: AP/Wide World Photos*

CHAPTER SIX

A Season to Remember

THERE WAS LITTLE DOUBT THAT MAGIC Johnson was joining the team steeped in a great basketball tradition. Thanks to their forerunners in Minneapolis years earlier, the franchise went back almost to the beginning of the NBA and had as storied a past as did the Boston Celtics, the team that Larry Bird had joined.

The Lakers originally played in the National Basketball League, a rival of the Basketball Association of America. It was the latter that was reorganized into the NBA in 1946. Two years later, when the NBL folded, the Lakers came into the NBA and won the championship five of the next six years. The leader of those Laker teams was 6'10" George Mikan, the NBA's first great big man. Mikan had help from the likes of Slater Martin, Jim

Pollard, Vern Mikkelsen, Clyde Lovellette, Dick Schnittker, and Whitey Skoog. They were a great team.

When the NBA went in search of large markets, the franchise was moved to Los Angeles before the start of the 1960–61 season. Right away there were a pair of resident superstars, forward Elgin Baylor and a rookie guard named Jerry West. Both are all-time greats, still considered among the best ever at their respective positions.

A year later the Lakers challenged the Bill Russell–Bob Cousy Celtics for the NBA title, losing in seven games. Five more times during the decade of the '60s the Lakers made it to the final round, only to be turned back by the Celtics each time. It had become a great rivalry. Toward the end of the decade center Wilt Chamberlain joined the Lakers to give the team its second great big man.

In 1969–70 L.A. lost yet another final round to the New York Knicks. It must have seemed as if they would never break through to bring that elusive championship to the City of Angels. Then in 1971–72 they finally made it, defeating the Knicks in five games to become world champs.

Baylor had retired nine games into the season, but Chamberlain was still there and even well into his thirties was still the best rebounder in the game. West and Gail Goodrich were a devastating backcourt combination, while Jim McMillian and Happy Hairston did the job up front. A very good Laker team, one that returned to the finals a year later only to lose to the Knicks.

Though the team continued to win after that, they never made it back to the final round, even with the arrival via a trade of Kareem Abdul-Jabbar in 1975–76. A 7'1" giant who was unanimously acknowledged as the best offensive player in the game, Abdul-Jabbar featured his famous "sky hook," a shot considered the most unstoppable (except for the slam dunk) in basketball history. Yet Abdul-Jabbar was often slammed for playing the game with a seeming nonchalance. He wasn't the defender or rebounder that Bill Russell and Chamberlain had been before him, though he was considered their successor as the game's dominant big man. But he still couldn't lead the Lakers back to the promised land.

In 1978–79 the Lakers finished third in the Pacific Division with a 47–35 record. But after beating the Denver Nuggets in a best-of-three first-round playoff series, the team was disposed of in just five games by the eventual champion Seattle. To some, it was a puzzle why this Laker team didn't fare better, especially during the playoffs when a superstar like Abdul-Jabbar should be able to dominate.

There were some other fine players on that ballclub. Forward Jamaal Wilkes was a smooth operator who averaged 18.6 points, second to Abdul-Jabbar's 23.8. Second-year point guard Norm Nixon looked like a coming star, while veteran forward Adrian Dantley was always a solid scorer. But the team lacked a power forward to support Kareem on the boards and didn't have enough good role players. And, as mentioned before, they seemed to lack a certain competitive fire, an on-court presence to drive them and pull them through the tough games. That's one reason the team drafted Earvin Johnson.

As always, Magic had planned a summer full of basketball. He played with some all-star teams, then came to Los Angeles to play a game with the Lakers summer league team. The game took place at the Cal State Los Angeles gym, where a normal crowd numbered about two or three hundred diehard fans. But on this night there were several thousand packed into the small gymnasium with several thousand more milling around outside, unable to get in. Nearly all of them were there to watch the smiling, enthusiastic rookie out of Michigan State.

Magic was pleasantly surprised by the huge turnout and he said later that it showed him that Los Angeles did indeed have good basketball fans. They were just waiting for something or someone to bring them out. Laker assistant coach Jack McCloskey was directing the summer league team and he chose not to start the youngster, who wasn't part of the regular group. The fans, of course, were there to see him.

It didn't take long, however, for McCloskey to get him in the game, and within a matter of minutes Magic was doing his thing. He handled the ball, directed the offense, hit the boards, and did some scoring in the twenty-eight minutes he played. It was enough to show everyone that he was the real thing. Now the excitement began to grow in earnest.

The Lakers made a coaching change before training camp began. Jerry West decided to step down and was replaced by Jack McKinney. At the time that didn't really matter to Magic. He just wanted to play and felt he could get along with any coach. But the appointment of McKinney was the first step in what would eventually become one of the most traumatic episodes in his basketball career. But not now.

Reality was the first trauma he had to face, the reality that it was time to leave his home and family in Lansing and go west. He would admit later that the prospect of living in Los Angeles frightened him a bit. After all, Lansing had retained much of a small-town atmosphere and in that sense Los Angeles must have seemed a world away.

If nothing else, the prices were. Magic's off-campus apartment at Michigan State had cost $250 a month. Similar apartments in L.A. went for four or five times as much. He was also shocked to find that even small condos started at about $200,000. Magic had a lot to learn, but that would come fast. To start, however, he simply took a small apartment near the L.A. airport.

Charles Tucker also spent a couple of weeks with him, helping him acclimate to his new home. He was also surprised to find that many people already knew him, recognized him on the street, wanted to get an autograph and talk basketball. That was fine with him. As always, he was friendly, smiling, and accommodating . . . and on his way to winning over an entire city.

When he joined the Lakers for training camp, he had to make a slight adjustment. He quickly realized he could not wear uniform number 33, as he had in college. There was a good reason for this. That number belonged to the big guy, Kareem. No way a raw rookie was going to ask a legend to give up his uniform. But that was no problem.

"I just switched to 32," he said. "I had worn both 32 and 33 in high school and took 33 at Michigan State because Kelser had 32."

Training camp was rough, the game much more physical than the one Magic had played in college. Guys were not only competing for jobs; they were competing for careers, livelihoods. So marginal players didn't go down without a fight, sometimes literally. But the hectic pace and bruising style was good in that it convinced Magic early on that he could handle the pro style. From there he just did his thing.

By the end of training camp he had beaten out veteran Ron Boone for the starting guard spot alongside Nixon. Kareem, of course, was in the middle, flanked by Jamaal Wilkes at one forward and veteran Jim Chones at the other. The team had also acquired veteran forward Spencer Haywood in a last-minute trade for

Adrian Dantley. He was expected to give the team a big lift off the bench. The opening game was against the San Diego Clippers at San Diego.

The game was supposed to be extraspecial because center Bill Walton was expected to be in the San Diego lineup. Walton had followed Abdul-Jabbar at UCLA and helped the Bruins continue their collegiate dominance. He had also led the Portland Trail Blazers to an NBA title in 1976–77. But a foot injury made Walton a scratch. Now the Clippers would have to rely on their high-scoring guard, Lloyd Free. The contest was shown on national television, with much of the attention on the professional debut of Magic Johnson.

It turned out to be a great game. The Clippers were playing in their own building and were sky-high. The Lakers were the team they took the most pleasure in beating and with Free hitting jump shots from all over the court, San Diego held the lead most of the way. In the fourth period the Clippers were still in front, but with Kareem doing his thing in the middle and Magic Johnson playing a great game in his professional debut, the Lakers edged closer and closer.

Magic looked poised and confident. He was handling the ball well, running the fast break, and setting up teammates with his crisp, accurate passes. He was also scoring well both from inside and out. What it came down to, however, was this. The Lakers trailed by a single point with time running out. All they could do was work for a final shot and hope they would hit.

Of course, the fairy-tale ending would have Magic taking—and making— that final shot. But when a team has Kareem Abdul-Jabbar and that sky hook, they would be crazy to do it any other way. Sure enough, Kareem got the ball to the right of the basket, turned his head, and brought his right arm high over his head. A flick of the wrist and the ball was headed downward toward the hoop. It kissed the net a split second before the buzzer sounded. The Lakers had won it by a point.

What followed officially ushered in a new era in Los Angeles Lakers basketball. Many times in the past a victory—even a dramatic one—was treated with a couple of high-fives, a slap or two on the back, all as the team walked slowly off the court. Not this time. Right after Kareem hit the winning shot, Magic Johnson rushed over and threw his arms around the veteran center, hugging him with joy, an ear-to-ear smile erupting on his face.

For a second neither Kareem nor the rest of the Lakers seemed to know how to react. Suddenly the big guy began grinning back, almost as widely as the rookie who was hugging him. Then all of the Lakers began celebrating, joining Magic in his jubilation as the television cameras took it all in. Who said the Lakers didn't show emotion? How could they not show it with Magic Johnson on the court? Oh, yes, Magic contributed in another way as well, scoring 26 points in his first NBA encounter.

There was a four-day gap before the next game. This one would be the home opener at the Forum and the Laker publicity people made it a gala event. Before the game several magicians were on hand to entertain the crowd. Get it? They were performing . . . magic. Glen Campbell was there to sing the National Anthem, while the University of Southern California Marching Band was also on hand. The opponents were the Chicago Bulls, the team that had lost the coin toss in the Magic Johnson sweepstakes.

It turned into another sweet victory for the Lakers. The now 6'8 1/2", 210-pound rookie put on a second fine performance. He had 19 points in that game, and for the two games had a total of 17 rebounds and 12 assists. He was proving to be everything his press clippings said he was. In addition, he seemed to be fitting in with his veteran Laker teammates without missing a beat. He himself said he was on such a high he didn't think he'd ever come down.

But sports is often a great equalizer. Playing against Seattle the very next night, Magic learned all over again how ephemeral a basketball career can be. He had a major league scare. Early in the game he went up for a rebound with Sonics center Jack Sikma. Their legs became entangled and both landed awkwardly. Magic felt the pain in his right knee immediately. He tried to get up, but the knee collapsed on him, the pain nearly unbearable.

His knee wrapped in ice before he was even helped from the floor, Magic was taken to the locker room where the Seattle team doctor came in and examined him. He asked about the pain, felt the knee, examined it some more, and then looked Magic directly in the eye.

"You have a partially torn ligament," he said. "My guess is you'll be out six to eight weeks, if all goes well."

The words came down on Magic with the force of a sledgehammer. Six to eight weeks! That was two months—and then only if all went well. Here he was, just three games into his rookie year and now this. He had never had a serious injury before, but he knew about ligament damage and knee injuries. Nothing was certain. The healing process differed from player to player. Some were never quite the same again.

Magic would say later that the pain in his knee was nothing compared to the pain he felt in his heart. The words "this isn't fair" flashed through his mind. It was as if his lifelong dream was being taken away before he even had a chance to enjoy it. Lying there in the locker-room as team trainer Jack Curran wrapped the knee tightly in a bandage, a myriad of mostly frightening thoughts ran through his mind.

He remembered when he was trying to decide whether to remain in school or turn pro. People had mentioned the injury factor, how a blown knee could blow a pro career. Now, three games into that pro career, he was dealing with a potentially serious knee injury. How ironic. Jack Curran tried to reassure him. He told Magic they would be seeing Dr. Robert Kerlan, the Lakers esteemed team physician, first thing in the morning. Maybe it wasn't as bad as it seemed.

Jerry Buss leased a private jet to get Magic back to L.A. as quickly as possible. The concern of Dr. Buss, his coaches, teammates, and friends amazed him. But it didn't make the knee feel any better. He spent the better part of the night on the telephone back to Lansing, talking with his parents and Charles Tucker. Mr. and Mrs. Johnson had been planning a Los Angeles trip to see him play. Magic told them to postpone it, but they refused. Charles Tucker told him that if it was a torn ligament, his youth would help it heal faster.

But none of that made him feel any better when he limped into Dr. Kerlan's office on crutches the next morning. Magic got on the table and Dr. Kerlan began looking at the knee. It took about an hour for the examination to be completed. Magic just lay there, eyes closed, wondering what the future held.

Then Dr. Kerlan began to massage the knee. As he did, he began to chuckle, then laugh. Magic opened his eyes and looked at the smiling man standing above him. He couldn't understand what was so funny. So he asked. With a smile still on his face, Dr. Kerlan joked about having to amputate the leg above the knee. Then he laughed again.

"You've got nothing wrong with your knee," he said. "It's just a sprain. You'll probably be playing again in a week."

Talk about words being music to the ears. This had to be a classic case. Magic was so elated he shouted for joy right in the doctor's office. It was the best possible news he could have heard. A week to ten days, tops. That meant he'd probably miss only three games. He could live with that, especially when it was juxtaposed against six to eight weeks and an uncertain future. Boy, could he ever live with that.

Sure enough, Dr. Kerlan's diagnosis was right on the money. Magic missed just three games, then returned to the lineup without missing a beat. During the next month or so, as the Lakers began getting deeper into their schedule, it was apparent they weren't the same team. They were winning and there was excitement. Coach McKinney noted how the front line had changed from the previous year, since Abdul-Jabbar, Wilkes, and Adrian Dantley were basically quiet people. Now the team had an infusion of . . . well, a little magic.

"The first thing Magic brought here was a big helping of enthusiasm and excitement," said the coach. "I think it's been infectious. It always helps, too, when a new player with the kind of advance press notices he had spends most of the game trying to pass the ball to his teammates. We had envisioned him as a terrific leader and ballhandler, but never thought of him as a scorer. But when he began scoring 30 and 40 points against NBA-caliber players during the summer, that's when we began to realize the full extent of his potential."

Now everyone was seeing it. Magic was beginning to put together some big games. In an overtime victory over Denver, he had 31 points, 8 assists, and 6 rebounds. In addition, he had 8 straight hoops during a late-game Laker rally, showing he could do it at crunch time. And the more the team ran, the better he seemed to be.

"When we starting running, really cranking it up, that's when my confidence soared," he said. "That's when I knew it was time to deal on some people. When we're rolling and the break is going, I guess it sometimes looks like I *am* performing magic out there. It's nights like that when I think I can do anything."

Others were also beginning to realize that this big kid with the perpetual grin was a very special kind of rookie.

"He has great charisma," said veteran guard Brian Taylor of San Diego. "It's fun to watch someone who can get the ball to his teammates when they're open. There are a few other players in the league who can do that, but what makes Magic special is the way he brings his own personality into it."

Even when the Lakers lost, as they did to Golden State, 126–109, Magic was impressing people. He called the game perhaps his least-inspired effort of the year, but Golden State coach and former NBA guard Al Attles also saw something special.

"There are two types of passers," Attles said. "One kind can make a pass that looks good but doesn't lead to anything. The second kind can get the ball to a teammate when he's in a position to do something with the ball. Magic is definitely the second kind."

Magic's first trip around the league continued to be an eventful one. Against San Diego he had 18 points, 9 rebounds, and 8 assists, and didn't commit a single turnover. Veteran forward Jim Chones, in his first year with the Lakers, saw a subtle difference between Magic and most of the other NBA guards.

"He sees angles a lot of other guards don't see," Chones explained. "Because of that he gives you the ball in the rhythm of your move so you can go right up with it."

Despite his talent, these things don't just happen. It's hard work and a cerebral approach to the game that enables Magic to blend his natural abilities into a complete game. He explained that he watched all of his new teammates very carefully during training camp, looking for the little nuances in their games that would help him to help them.

"I tried to pay attention to tendencies," he said. "If I'm going to throw a no-look pass, I want to be sure somebody's going to catch it. I messed up a lot of times in training camp and in the preseason, even hit people in the face at first. But I worked at it until I got it right."

He was getting plenty right. After twelve games Magic was averaging a surprising 20.3 points a game and hitting 55 percent of his shots. Remember how they said he couldn't shoot? He was doing a lot of the damage inside, taking high-percentage shots, but it was his skills that got him inside. He was using his height and long arms to take advantage of smaller guards, who had trouble keeping up with him in the paint. There was also little doubt that Magic was affecting the team. The club already had a 9–1 record at the Forum and was leading their division. It was a combination of both his physical and his emotional presence that was getting the job done.

During his long NBA career, which began back in 1969, Kareem Abdul-Jabbar was often known as an unemotional player, a guy who was sometimes aloof with his teammates. There was no denying his talent and desire to win, but it often didn't appear that way to the fans, and maybe even to some of his teammates. But the big guy came to camp ready in 1979. He was more muscular (the result of a weight training program) and more animated on the court.

"It's not Kareem's way to be jumping up and down all the time," said Norm Nixon, "but you can tell he's more enthusiastic now."

Magic himself said it was very important for him to feel accepted by Kareem, the player he called the franchise.

"I had heard he was unemotional, that he didn't work hard," said Magic. "But the stories I heard weren't true. Kareem cracked jokes, got mad, and worked hard. The guy has got feelings."

Many felt that it was the rookie Johnson who accounted for the subtle change in Abdul-Jabbar. Sure, the incredible sky hook was always going to be there, but when the sky hook had an occasional smile behind it, or a high five, or the pumping of a fist, then it meant just a little more to everyone. The big guy must have read the stories about Magic, then saw the enthusiasm for himself. Some of it had to be catching. After all, how can you ignore a player who says: "You really have to love the game. You can't be afraid to let your emotions out in front of 13,000 people."

Holding back his emotions was something Magic Johnson never did.

Magic wasn't the only good news the NBA had at the outset of the 1979–80 season. If the league needed an infusion of talented, charismatic new blood, they were getting not one, but two. At the same time Magic was making his auspicious debut with the Lakers, the Bird man was doing the same thing with the Celtics. Boston had made a rare visit to the basement the season before, having a disastrous 29–53 year. Now, with the rookie Bird in the lineup, the Celts had recaptured their traditional winning ways to the point of battling for first place in their division.

Like Magic across the continent, Bird was doing everything he had done in college without missing a beat. He was scoring, rebounding, making his brilliant passes, and generally raising the level of play of the veterans around him, players who had looked tired and uncompetitive a year earlier. So the NBA had a pair of crown jewels and the league's public relations department was making the most of it.

Wouldn't it be great, more than one person said, if Magic and Bird wound up in the NBA's championship series just a year after meeting for the NCAA title? If it happened, it would be a public relations coup, and the way both ballclubs were going, it appeared to be a definite possibility.

But the NBA season is a long one and as Magic already learned with his knee scare, anything can happen. With the Lakers, something totally unexpected did occur early in the season, something that would affect Magic, the other players, and the entire future course of the team.

It happened some ten days after Magic returned from his knee injury and just thirteen games into the season. It was an off day and Coach McKinney was on his way to play a round of tennis with assistant coach Paul Westhead. A physical fitness buff, McKinney was riding a bicycle to the tennis courts when he took a bad fall. He suffered serious head injuries and had to be hospitalized. Since he would be unable to coach for an undetermined period of time, Paul Westhead took over the team.

A few weeks later when it became apparent that McKinney might not be able to coach for the remainder of the season, Westhead was named the interim head coach. Shortly after that he asked Pat Riley to come down to the bench as his assistant. Riley had been an All-American at Kentucky and had a marginal career in the NBA, including a stint with the Lakers where he was a dependable role player. In 1979 he was beginning his third season as the color man to Chick Hearn on Laker broadcasts. When Westhead asked him to be his assistant, Riley quickly accepted.

Westhead was an introspective, intelligent man who

had lectured in college and earned a reputation as a Shakespearean scholar. It would come as no surprise if he had his own coaching ideas and style. But with the team going so well and the chemistry apparently in place, Westhead didn't rock the boat. He continued to use the same basic system that Jack McKinney had instituted and his laissez-faire approach to the team earned him the respect of the players almost immediately. In other words, the unexpected coaching change presented no problems.

The biggest adjustment for Magic as a rookie was playing in the same backcourt with Norm Nixon. Both were point guards and used to handling the basketball. It doesn't take a mathematical genius to realize that two into one won't go. Two players, one basketball. They can't both have it at once. Both Jack McKinney and Paul Westhead preferred that they shared the ball, rather than turning one of them into the off guard or shooting guard.

Magic admitted that the two didn't click immediately. Both were used to getting the basketball as soon as the team went on offense and the one without the ball must have felt as if part of his body was missing. Nixon, for instance, wasn't used to working with a big guard who could rebound like a forward. When Magic would get a rebound, Nixon would cut into the middle for an outlet pass, the right move for point guard.

But Magic had been rebounding like a big man all his life and was accustomed to taking the ball straight down the middle himself to start the fast break. Nixon, then, had to get used to moving without the ball. If he got himself into a good position quickly, Magic would get the pass to him for an open jump shot.

There were still times during those first few months when the two backcourtmen would be out of sync and actually run into each other. That meant many hours of talk and analysis until both players understood each other's game. Instinct had to take over. If Nixon had it, Magic would have to get out fast and run downcourt. When Magic rebounded or took an outlet pass, Nixon learned to get out of there and look for a seam from which he could get an open shot. As Magic said: "By the end of the season we were really clicking and played beautifully together."

During the second half of the season the Lakers were even better. From the end of January through the completion of the regular schedule, the team won 23 games and lost only 5. Not even the unexpected coaching change slowed the ballclub down. The only conflict on the team was when Coach Westhead couldn't seem to settle on Jim Chones or Spencer Haywood as his starting power forward. First it was Chones, then Haywood, and finally Chones again. That caused some tense moments, but otherwise it was a grand season.

The Lakers finished the year as Pacific Division champs by four games over Seattle, winding up with a 60–22 record, a 13-game improvement over the season before. And as the playoffs approached, Norm Nixon spoke for a lot of the Lakers when he said, "I don't see anybody beating us."

As for Magic, he had an absolutely brilliant first season. At mid-year he became the first rookie since Elvin Hayes in 1969 to start in the All-Star Game. And when the year ended, he had done better than anyone had expected. In 77 games he averaged 18.0 points, had 596 rebounds and 563 assists. He shot 53 percent from the field and 81 percent from the free-throw line. And none of that mentions the intangibles he brought to the team.

With the playoffs set to begin, it was looking as if there might be a Johnson–Bird matchup in the finals after all. Bird had led the Celtics to a divisional title with a 61–21 record, the biggest single-season turnaround in NBA history to date. The Celts won by two games over the 76ers and even had a better record (by one game) than the Lakers.

Bird continued to be the co-featured story of the year in the NBA. He, too, had a sensational rookie season, playing in all 82 games and averaging 21.3 points a game. He also had 852 rebounds and 370 assists. Plus he had the same effect on his team as Magic did. He made the other guys wake up and smell the roses . . . but only if they hustled and played up to their full ability.

These two great rookies received nothing but praise all year long and at the same time gave the NBA a semblance of class that it had been missing—justifiably so or not—for several years. For example, both teams played late February games against different opponents on the same night. L.A. beat Denver, 116–103, as Magic led the Lakers with 30 points and 12 rebounds, as well as put on a dazzling passing performance in the second half as his club overcame a 57–53 halftime deficit.

"If you look at his nickname, 'Magic,' you would think all he does is make fancy passes," said Coach Westhead. "But he's as much a bread-and-butter guard as he is a passer. He'll take the ball down the lane in traffic and he'll also rebound. That's why he's so respected by his teammates. He gets down in the trenches, too, but he can still make the Bob Cousy–type pass."

That same night the Celtics whipped the Utah Jazz, 105–98, as Bird scored 33 points to lead both clubs.

"Bird is a great player already," said Utah coach Tom Nissalke. "He's the best to come into the pros since Bill Walton."

Many apparently agreed with Nissalke. For at the end of the season it would be Larry Bird once again edging Magic for a major award. The year before Larry had been college basketball's Player of the Year over Magic. Now he would be named Rookie of the Year in the NBA, with Magic finishing a close second. So the two players' names continued to be linked. What would happen come playoff time?

The Lakers started in fine fashion, rolling over the Phoenix Suns in just five games. The team looked powerful and confident. Magic and Norm Nixon had truly become a formidable backcourt. The number-three guard, Michael Cooper, was a tenacious defensive player, a great leaper and streak shooter. When he was in the game, Magic often worked with him the same way he had worked with Greg Kelser at Michigan State. One passes, the other dunks.

Jamaal Wilkes was a high-scoring forward capable of the real big night at any time. Chones could rebound well and was also a tough defensive player. Abdul-Jabbar was himself, the most formidable scoring threat in the middle who ever played.

Next came defending champion Seattle. The series opened at the Forum and the Supersonics played extremely well in the first game, winning it on a Jack Sikma free throw with just two seconds left. But the Lakers evened things up in game two, then won the third and the fourth in Seattle. In game four L.A. trailed by 21 points midway through the third period before they really got their running game in gear. Led by Magic, Nixon, and the rest, they won by 5, totally demoralizing the Sonics. That paved the way for another victory in game five and it was on to the finals. Just a year away from Michigan State and a national title, Magic Johnson would be playing for an NBA championship.

Unfortunately for basketball purists, there would be no dream matchup. The Celtics were upset by arch-rival Philadelphia in the Eastern Conference finals in just five games. So the Lakers would be going up against Philadelphia for the NBA title. And before the best-of-seven series was over, Earvin Johnson would be adding to the growing legend of Magic in just his rookie year.

The 76ers were led by a legend of their own, the great forward Julius Erving. Doctor J, as he was called, was a singularly explosive player who could do more things in the air than most players could do on the ground. The Doc played in the old American Basketball Association his first few years out of college and that's when he was really turned loose. In the ABA the Doctor routinely made the spectacular the norm. After the ABA folded he was signed by the Sixers prior to the 1976–77 season. Erving toned down his game somewhat in the NBA but was coming off a great year and was still capable of taking over a ballgame offensively.

The rest of the Philly front line was also tough. There was 7'0" Caldwell Jones and 6'11" Darryl Dawkins playing together up front. Jones was a fine defensive player, Dawkins a mountain of a man who often bounced bodies, shattered backboards, and could still bury a jumper. His problem was inconsistency. The speedy Bobby Jones and the rugged Steve Mix were outstanding backups.

Point guard Maurice Cheeks was a second-year player who ran the offense well. He was no Magic Johnson, but was a more than capable leader. The loss to injury of shooting guard Doug Collins hurt, but veteran Henry Bibby was still capable of playing solid ball. And, hey, this team had upset the Celtics and Larry Bird. So they were no pushovers.

The championship series opened at the Forum in Los Angeles before a large and noisy crowd. Magic and his teammates did their thing, but they could also see right away that the Sixers wouldn't rattle. No team that had a player as great as Julius Erving would fold up its tent. The Doctor, like Magic and Larry Bird, was one of those special players who always brought his teammates' level of play up a notch or two. But L.A. hung on down the stretch to take the opener, 109–102.

They found out in the second game, however, that the Sixers meant business. Darryl Dawkins, the twenty-three-year-old manchild, who had virtually disappeared in eighteen minutes of action in the first game, became a one-man wrecking crew in the second. Playing for forty-one minutes, young Dawkins scored 26 points, including 8 straight at the beginning of the third quarter to help turn the game around. Philly won it, 107–104, to even the series and take away the home-court advantage from the Lakers.

It was not a good night for L.A. on another front. Spencer Haywood had been carping about playing time and not getting along with Coach Westhead. During the Philadelphia victory, Haywood was becoming a distraction, encouraging fans to cheer for him and standing on the outside fringe of the team huddles. After the game Westhead suspended Haywood for the remainder of the season citing "activities disruptive toward the team."

The rest of the Lakers had to forget about it and concentrate on basketball. That's what they did, regaining the home-court advantage with a 111–101 victory at the Spectrum in Philadelphia. But when the Sixers won game four, 105–102, it began to look like a seven-game struggle was in the offing. Three of the first four games were decided by 7 points or less, the other by 10. The fifth game would be pivotal.

Before game five there was another announcement from the Laker front office. It said that Jack McKinney would not be returning as coach the next year. McKinney had apparently recovered from his injuries, but with Westhead leading the club into the finals, owner Buss decided not to make a change. Again, the timing of the announcement upset some of the Lakers.

In the fifth game Kareem Abdul-Jabbar was at his best. The sky hook was on target and neither Caldwell Jones nor Dawkins could stop it. But even with Kareem doing his thing, the Lakers couldn't pull away from the doggedly determined Sixers. Then, toward the end of the third period, Abdul-Jabbar pulled up lame with a bad sprain of the left ankle.

Between periods trainer Jack Curran taped the ankle tightly and Kareem appeared ready for the final session. All the big guy did was score another 14 points, then win it with a dunk and a free throw in the closing seconds to put the icing on a 108–103 victory. Los Angeles was just a game away from a world championship as Kareem finished with 40 big points.

That was the good news. The bad news came after the game. When the doctors examined Kareem's ankle, they said the sprain was too severe for him to play in game six. He would remain behind in Los Angeles with the hope that constant treatment would have him ready for at least limited duty if there was a seventh game.

Kareem's absence presented a definite problem for the Lakers. For starters, he averaged 33.4 points, 13.6 rebounds, and 4.6 blocks in the first five games. Without him, Jones and Dawkins would seem like a pair of twin towers, and Erving was capable of flying over both of them. Without the big guy to block the middle, it looked as if the Lakers were in big trouble.

The situation was reminiscent of something that had happened back in the finals in 1969–70. The New York Knicks were playing the Lakers then and in game five Knick center Willis Reed severely injured his hip. The New Yorkers rallied and won the game but then lost the sixth game when Reed didn't play. In the seventh game Reed made just a token appearance, but the Knicks played inspired, intense basketball and won anyway, defeating Wilt Chamberlain and the Lakers by using speed to control the tempo of the game.

Maybe Paul Westhead thought about that situation. Logic said that Jim Chones, who had played center earlier in his career, would move into the middle. Then maybe Magic could move up to forward with Michael Cooper taking his spot alongside Nixon in the backcourt. But before boarding the plane to Philadelphia, the coach walked up to his great rookie and said: "You're the starting center tomorrow night, E.J."

At first, Magic thought the coach was joking. But he went along with it by sitting in the seat usually reserved for Kareem and teasing the rest of his teammates. It wasn't until the team got to Philly and began practicing that Magic realized Westhead was serious. He found himself running a number of plays in the pivot.

"The Sixers better be ready for us," Magic said in the locker room before the game. "They're gonna see the new Lakers tonight."

Philadelphia fans licked their chops at the prospect of playing the Lakers without Kareem. When the players took the court, sure enough there was Magic Johnson lining up to jump center against seven-footer Caldwell Jones.

"I looked at Caldwell and realized that with his height and long arms he must have been about 9'5"," Magic said. "So I just decided to jump up and down quick, then work on the rest of my game."

That game quickly helped produce a 7–0 lead. Once the Sixers cut it to 7–4, Magic went to work. First he threw a pass to Cooper from the high post that led to a basket. Next he muscled for position, grabbed a rebound, dribbled the length of the court, and hit a jumper. On the next series he drove past Doctor J and canned a bank shot. Next he drove the lane, thought about dunking, then saw big Darryl Dawkins swinging over to defend.

It was back to hoopsy-doopsy days. He faked Dawkins, double-pumped, hung in the air, made the shot . . . and drew a foul! In a nutshell, he was doing it all. But once the early run was over, the Sixers bounced back. To their credit, they didn't panic, just kept playing their game. With Erving and Steve Mix going inside, the Sixers took the lead and pulled ahead, 52–44. Then the Lakers rebounded and at the half the game was tied at 60–60. It was still up for grabs.

Magic came out and hit the first hoop of the second half. It was followed by a basket by Cooper, then by Wilkes. Cooper got another, so did Wilkes. Then Magic hit again, and then Wilkes once more. Fourteen straight points and a 74–60 lead. But it wasn't over yet. In the fourth quarter the Sixers battled back, making it a 2-point game at 103–101 with 5:12 left. Westhead called time out.

"I was tired at that point," Magic said. "Really tired. But I had no choice. I had to go back out there and run through it."

Again Magic positioned himself under the hoop. Cooper missed a jumper and Magic was right there to tip it in. Then Wilkes connected on a drive, was fouled, and hit the free throw. In a flash the lead was up to 7. All within 1:16 of the time-out. The Sixers tried to close again, but in the final 2:22 Magic took over. He scored 9 points in the closing minutes to put the game and the championship on ice. The Lakers had won it, 123–107, and they did it without their big man.

When the final numbers were in they were hard to believe. Magic Johnson had put together one of the great games of all time. He finished the night with 42 points, hitting 14 of 23 shots from the field and a perfect 14 for 14 from the foul line. On top of that he had 15 rebounds, 7 assists, 3 steals, and a blocked shot. It was hard to envision anyone playing a better game, let alone a twenty-year-old rookie. The Sixers found his performance tough to believe.

"I knew he was good, but I never realized he was

great," said injured guard Doug Collins. "You don't realize it because he gives up so much of himself for Kareem."

Julius Erving, who maybe knew better than anyone about brilliant performances, said that "Magic was outstanding. Unreal."

In the locker room it was announced that Magic had been chosen the MVP of the finals. Yet when one of the announcers interviewing him mentioned that it was one of the quietest locker rooms he had ever been in, Magic said, "If you ran up and down the court the way we did for 48 minutes nonstop, you'd be kind of quiet, too."

Almost overlooked because of Magic's majestical performance was how the rest of the Lakers came through. Wilkes also played his best game ever, with 37 points and 10 rebounds. Chones had 11 points and 10 rebounds. Sub forward Mark Landsberger had 10 rebounds in nineteen minutes, as L.A. dominated the boards. Cooper used his speed to play great defense and score 16 points. The name of the game when played right, as always, was team. And with Magic it was spelled with a capital *T*. His enthusiasm and intensity had spread to the entire team.

After the game, Paul Westhead smiled and shook his head when asked for the umpteenth time about the way Magic played.

"Magic thinks every season goes like that," he said. "You play some games, win the title, and get named MVP."

The Bubble Bursts

I T HAD REALLY BEEN A MAGICAL RIDE, almost like a fairytale. How could any-one have scripted it better? From NCAA champion to NBA champion in one year. MVP both times. Plaudits and accolades at every turn. Magic probably could have run for mayor of Los Angeles and even the popular Tom Bradley would have been in trouble. Maybe the toughest question someone could have asked Magic right then and there was, *hey, what can you do for an encore?*

The answer, however, would have been simple for him. *Keep on winning.* That's what the game is all about, and the only way he knew how to play. So when he went to his second Laker training camp, he came in with the same attitude and enthusiasm of the year before. Work hard, improve your game, blend in with your teammates, and get the job done.

More than one reporter, used to dealing with professional athletes who were sometimes moody and sullen, asked Magic how he could stay so upbeat and keep a smile on his face.

"I guess I've been blessed," Magic said, on more than one occasion. "The strength comes from my father, the smile from my mother. But this was always me long before I got all this attention. I've always had it and it goes all the way back to first grade. You can ask anyone in Lansing. They all know me."

At the start of the 1980–81 season Magic and his Laker teammates had a new goal. No NBA team had won back-to-back championships since the Boston Celtics of 1968 and 1969. This team seemed fully capable of doing it. The chemistry was there. Magic was a year older, a year more experienced, and even more assured of his skills. Not surprisingly, the team came out of the gate fast. They looked great.

On November 11, the Lakers were in Atlanta to play the Hawks. Atlanta center Tom Burleson, a 7'4" giant, was wearing a heavy protective knee brace that had two iron bars on each side. During the course of the game, there was a pileup underneath the basket. Burleson fell on top of Magic and the knee brace raked across Magic's left knee.

Magic said the knee felt strange when he got up. It didn't really hurt, so he continued playing. Most athletes become accustomed to playing with all kinds of bumps and bruises, even with pulled muscles, a broken jaw, cracked ribs. With the team going so well, the last thing Magic wanted to do was sit out. So he stayed in the lineup. Then, five nights later, he collided with Tom LaGarde of the Mavericks and banged the knee up again.

This time he noticed a little clicking noise in the knee. It clicked with each step, but because the knee still didn't hurt he continued. Shortly after, the knee began to stiffen. Finally, in a game with Kansas City, Magic made a sharp cut and heard a snap inside the knee. Now he knew something was definitely wrong. Dr. Kerlan examined it and told Magic that he had torn cartilage. He recommended immediate surgery with the hope there was no damage also done to the ligament.

If it was just torn cartilage, Magic would most likely be back before the playoffs, and with no permanent problems with the knee. But that didn't comfort him. The team was off to a 15–5 start and Magic was tenth in the league in scoring with a 21.4 average. He was also leading the league in both steals and assists, while his 8.2 rebounding average was best among the league's guards. There was no denying that he was having an All-Star-caliber season.

He had also never been seriously hurt before. That, too, made it difficult. But a knee injury cannot be ignored, so Magic followed Dr. Kerlan's advice and had the operation. With their point guard out of the lineup, the Lakers lost five of their next eight games. They missed him and he, in turn, missed them.

"It made me see that just as fast as you can rise to the top, you can come tumbling down," Magic said. "You lose the ball and you lose being around your teammates. That really hurts. I've always enjoyed the entire experience of basketball, being part of a team. All of a sudden that's taken away. You're alone trying to get better, and that's not easy."

The first two weeks after surgery, Magic had to wear a cast on the entire leg. That was tough. When the cast came off and Magic had regained some mobility, he decided to go to the Forum and sit on the bench with the team. This was right after the club had lost five of eight, an un-Lakerlike occurrance that prompted Coach Westhead to make some changes. He decided to bench both Michael Cooper, who had taken Magic's place in the starting lineup, and Jim Chones. Both players accepted the change very badly and fumed because the coach wouldn't explain the reason for the move. Magic noticed it that night. Things weren't the same.

Magic would say later that Coach Westhead wasn't communicating with the guys. The move to change the lineup and shake up the team might not have been a bad one, but the coach owed his players the common courtesy of an explanation, if nothing else. After that, though, the team came back to win five in a row, then dropped five of eight, before taking seventeen of the next twenty-four. When Magic finally returned on February 27, the Lakers had gone 28–17 without him. Not great, but far from being bad. They were second to Phoenix in the Pacific Division.

"He's just one guy," Kareem Abdul-Jabbar said, when someone asked him about life without Magic. "He's special with great instincts and ability, but we're a team."

Magic worked harder than he ever had in his life to rehabilitate the knee and get ready to play again. It involved a strict daily regimen of sweat and toil, much of it done alone. Assistant Coach Pat Riley also helped him, pushing and prodding, making him work and work and work. When he finally returned, there were just seventeen games left before the playoffs. But Magic knew he was ready. The knee felt fine.

Interestingly, attendance at the Forum was down during Magic's absence. That couldn't have made his teammates feel too good about themselves. When the date for his return was announced, the Lakers were determined to make it an gala affair. There would be

"The Magic Is Back" buttons passed out to every fan at the game and a full house was expected. A pair of Magic Johnson Jogging Suits would also be given away, almost like a door prize. Magic was already endorsing a whole group of products and it was difficult to go anywhere in L.A. without seeing or hearing him.

"The thing that amazes me about Magic is his timing," said Jamaal Wilkes. "He's always in the right place at the right time. . . . Look at him now, coming back a month before the playoffs. The spotlight is all his. Nobody on the team resents him at all. We love him. The only athlete I've ever seen who is like him is [Muhammad] Ali."

But below the surface there were some rumblings, though they stayed buried for a short time. There was no reason for anyone to think the Laker boat was rocking. Magic admitted he was nervous before his return, almost like it was a first game. There was a sellout crowd of 17,505 on hand to see the Lakers play the lowly New Jersey Nets, and they weren't all there to see the Nets. When Magic was announced, the first Laker to come on the court, the crowd went wild. It was literally the second coming, because to the fans at the Forum, Magic was the savior. The cheering didn't stop. Some of his teammates shook their heads and Magic himself was a little embarrassed.

He didn't start the game, but Westhead put him in late in the first quarter. His first pass was picked off, his second went out of bounds. Then his first two shots missed badly. The entire team was flat, though they still managed to win against the Nets. As soon as he got in there, Magic noticed that he and Norm Nixon seemed out of synch again. He was surprised, but in his absence Nixon had gotten used to having the ball again. The two would have to spend some time readjusting and getting it together once more.

In the closing weeks of the regular season Magic said he began to get the impression that he was odd man out. For some reason, he didn't feel like one of the guys anymore and found that difficult to accept. Maybe it was because he'd been away from the team for so long. He didn't know, and didn't have time to think about it. He just wanted to get back in the groove and ready for the playoffs. As the regular season ended, he felt he was doing it.

The team finished with a 54–28 record, second to Phoenix in the Pacific Division. Their first taste of playoff action would be against the Houston Rockets in a best-of-three miniseries. But before that started, the harmony on the ballclub was tested again. A newspaper story in Los Angeles quoted Norm Nixon as saying that Magic's presence took something away from his game. It also said that Magic not only hogged the ball, but publicity and endorsements as well.

When reporters asked him about it, Magic answered by saying that the Lakers were becoming a bunch of individuals, which was strange, because a year earlier no one had had ego problems. He also reminded everyone that he hadn't gone to the companies; they'd come to him. And he didn't write the stories; members of the press did. As a result, when the team got set to face the Rockets, the locker room was filled with talk of an incipient feud.

What followed was a terrible series that the Lakers lost in three games. In the third and final contest, Magic was just 2 for 14 from the field. Then, with the Lakers trailing by one in the final seconds, Westhead diagrammed a play designed to get the ball to Kareem for the final shot that could win the game. As the clock ticked down, Magic had the ball at the top of the key. But instead of passing inside, he tried an off-balance shot. It was an air ball, Houston got the rebound, and the Lakers lost.

"It was the worst game of my life," Magic said later, admitting that his head wasn't in it because of all the extra-curricular dissension. He also explained that on the final play he felt he couldn't get the ball in to Kareem because of a double-team and that he made an instinctive, split-second decision to shoot. Magic understood that no one can win them all. But did everyone else?

For the first time since joining the Lakers, Magic took a beating in the press. There were stories that the magic was gone and one article even went so far as to refer to him as "Tragic" Johnson. A bit much, but reporters sometimes tend to try to outdo their competitors with a turn of phrase, just as ballplayers try to top the competition on the court. And for some reason, the sports world has always been quick to create a "yesterday's hero."

Magic had missed forty-five games due to the knee injury, but still averaged 21.6 points for the thirty-seven games in which he played. He had to sit back, however, and watch Larry Bird lead the Celtics to the NBA crown, undoubtedly wondering whether they would have met in the final round had he not been injured. The interesting part was that the two super rookies of 1979 had now both led their respective teams to a championship. They had certainly been impact players and were responsible for a great deal of renewed interest in the NBA. Magic Johnson and Larry Bird had become the two top attractions in the league.

But Magic couldn't think about that now. Instead he had to deal with the problems building up within his own team. The season might have ended, but not the turmoil. It would get worse before it got better. Shortly after the season ended, owner Buss sat down with Magic and asked him point-blank if he and Nixon could play together. Magic said yes, that Nixon's remarks in the paper had supposedly been taken out of context and he would rather play alongside Norm than with any other guard in the league.

Buss then got the two guards together and they all discussed the situation. Nixon, too, said he and Magic could work it out. Everyone agreed. But that wasn't the end of Magic's problems. A few weeks after the season ended, he signed a new contract. It was a unique kind of deal and one that would again create problems within the team.

According to Magic, the team owner had begun discussing a contract extension the previous summer. Dr. Buss had already extended the contracts of several Lakers, including Nixon, Wilkes, and Michael Cooper. Until then, Magic had always thought about returning to the Midwest at some point in his career, finishing things up in his own backyard, in a sense. So when Jerry Buss began talking extension, Magic was thinking in terms of one or two years.

Discussions with Magic's attorneys eventually produced a rather unique idea—a lifetime contract. When the Laker owner came back with the numbers, everyone was flabbergasted. At the time it was the richest and longest-running contract in the history of sports. Dr. Buss was offering Magic a $25 million, twenty-five-year contract.

The contract was signed shortly after the 1980–81 season ended. Exact terms were not supposed to be revealed. But these things have a way of slipping out and pretty soon there were rumors that Magic was making more money than Kareem, which would violate an unwritten rule on the club. The big guy was supposed to be the highest-paid player. Dr. Buss then revealed the terms of the contract, adding that it was a personal-services contract guaranteed by Buss, not the Laker team, and that Magic would continue to work for him once his playing days ended.

Well, the whole thing suddenly exploded as if a bomb had been dropped. Magic was back home in Michigan when the story broke and he was shocked. But apparently Buss thought the terms of the contract had already leaked out and he was only confirming them. Magic said there were some misconceptions. First of all, the new pact didn't go into effect until his original five-year deal ended in 1984. He also explained that he was not obligated to Dr. Buss for twenty-five years. That was only the length of the payout. He also had not become part of management, as rumored, and there was no preset agreement for him to someday take over as coach, general manager, or even team president.

The person most concerned by Magic's contract and the ensuing stories was Abdul-Jabbar. A short time after the announcement there were more rumors, this time that Kareem had requested a trade to New York, his hometown. Apparently, there was a feeling that Dr. Buss was singling Magic out as his favorite, a kind of teacher's pet, that there could well be a kind of double-standard where Magic was concerned. Buss tried to assure Kareem that Magic was subject to the same rules as everyone else. There was no favoritism intended and none existed.

Magic was so upset by the entire situation that he threatened to tear up the new contract. He told the press that he was not in the game strictly for the money and wasn't a greedy person. Anyone who knew Magic also knew he was being completely truthful. His love of the game and of being part of a cohesive, smooth-working, no-ego-problem winning team were the things that meant the most to him. Sure, he'd become a shrewd businessman surrounded by very solid advisors. Why shouldn't he, especially in the economic climate that was quickly escalating in the early 1980s? But the game itself was always number one with him. That would never change.

Once training camp opened, things appeared to mellow out. Little did Magic know, however, that the problems were not over yet. There would be still another major hurdle put directly in his path shortly after the new season began. Paul Westhead was beginning his third year as Laker coach, his second full season, and, according to Magic, the coach had lost almost all personal contact with the team. No longer did he want or accept input from the players. It was his way or no way.

Westhead greeted the team with a new offense, designed to go almost exclusively to Kareem. That was the first option every time down court. But as Magic noted, defenses quickly began clogging the middle, and this made it increasingly difficult for the other Lakers to get the ball inside. Westhead also instituted a series of picks, or screens, ostensibly designed to help get the ball inside. But the offense wasn't working. As Magic said, "It immobilized us."

Most of the players loved the running game. They felt the team was at its best as a breaking, running, speed team. The slower, half-court-type offense wasn't Laker basketball. Whenever Magic or Nixon tried to create something different, the coach would castigate them, tell them they weren't running the offense. When they told him the offense wasn't working, he'd snap back that if they ran it correctly, it would work.

Then the coach began calling plays from the bench. As soon as the Lakers got the ball, Westhead would stand up and signal one of two plays, both set up for Kareem. The play-calling also completely eliminated the break, because when either Magic or Nixon had to hold up and look to the bench, any chance to run was almost gone.

The team was not playing well as the 1981–82 season started. Even when they won, they looked sluggish and slow. Still, Westhead wouldn't budge from his offense. He just kept tinkering with it, making some slight adjustments, nothing more. The players weren't happy, but the coach would hear none of it. In a November 10 game against San Antonio, the Lakers were beaten by twenty-six points. Magic said he felt "humiliated," adding he had never been on a team that played so poorly. At that point, the team record had dropped to 2–4.

Magic got word to Jerry Buss that he wasn't happy with the way the team was playing. He stopped short of asking to be traded, but admitted he was thinking about it and thinking about it seriously. The problems continued. Whenever the players started to speak up, the coaches stopped them. This wasn't a good situation. As Magic said, "Players have a feel for the game, a feel for what's happening on the court that the coaches cannot possibly have."

It was later learned that Buss had already decided to fire Westhead. After the loss to San Antonio, the owner said, "There was a lack of excitement on offense that I wanted to see. I want to see a fluid team on the floor. I enjoyed 'Showtime' and I want to see it again. I'm speaking as much as a fan as anything else."

Dr. Buss wanted Jerry West to return as coach. West, who was then a special consultant, didn't want the job again. Meanwhile the situation between coach and players got worse. And so did Magic's frustration. Buss, incidentally, gave his reason as uninspired victories over inferior opposition. Though the club had won a couple after the San Antonio game, they still looked sluggish and uninspired. The fans in L.A. were used to a winner, and used to exciting basketball.

Everything came to a head after a 113–110 victory

over Utah. It was the Lakers' fifth straight win following the 2–4 start, but even the victories came hard and weren't pretty. After the game, Magic got into it with Westhead, who said he didn't like Magic's attitude during a huddle, or his lack of concentration. And, again, the whole thing came down to a matter of not running the offense.

Magic would say later that his attitude had never before been questioned and he had never been accused of not listening to a coach. Or, to simply sum it up, he said, "The game is my life."

He had finally had enough. The other players were still in the lockerroom when Magic said, to no one in particular, that it was over. He told his teammates he loved them and had had fun, but he was out of there. He had decided to ask for a trade. Minutes later he was telling the press the same thing.

As soon as Jerry Buss found out what happened he called Jerry West and general manager Bill Sharman together. They knew the timing would be bad, but decided to make a change immediately. West still didn't want the job and talked Buss into making Pat Riley the interim coach with West on the bench as a temporary assistant. Buss told them he didn't care what kind of arrangement Riley and West had, as long as West put the excitement back in the offense and got it moving again.

Buss personally called Magic to inform him about the change. The owner said he had noticed the offense bogging down in the playoff loss to Houston the season before, and had initially thought about replacing Westhead after the Rockets again topped the Lakers in the opening game of the season. What he was telling Magic, basically, was that it wasn't his fault the coach was being fired.

Unfortunately, it didn't appear that way to the press

and much of the public. For the first time in his career, Earvin Johnson was being viewed as something other than a smiling, happy guy who loved to play basketball. One story asked if a "20-year-old who had the ability to make everyone smile just by walking into a room . . . had turned into a greedy, petulant, and obnoxious 22-year-old?"

Magic countered by saying, "I'm here to play ball and have fun, and that hasn't been happening. But I'm not here to get anyone fired. I'm not management. I'm just a player like everyone else."

But was he? Some people came right out and said it: *Magic Johnson got Paul Westhead fired.* It was the old teacher's pet theory again. Magic whined and Jerry Buss reacted. After all, the team was 7–4 with Magic averaging 17.4 points, a league-best ten assists and three steals a game.

Westhead, for his part, seemed shocked by the news. "I thought we were becoming an excellent team," he said.

Jerry Buss tried to diffuse another potentially explosive situation by explaining that Westhead would have been gone anyway, even if Magic hadn't asked to be traded. But, unfortunately, some of the Lakers didn't see it that way. Jamaal Wilkes, for one, said he was shocked by Magic's statements, adding, "If [Magic] got mad at a player, would the player be gone the next day?"

So once again, Magic Johnson was being thrust into the role as the heavy. Yet all the players, almost to a man, hated Westhead's offense. The team was in turmoil, not playing to one of its strong suits and, according to player reports, the coach would not accept any input from others. It sounded as if the situation could only get worse. Even Sharman and West supposedly felt that Westhead was forcing players with particular talents to fit into a system, instead of devising a system to fit the players' talents. Yet it was Magic who was taking the heat. In fact, he was really crucified in some circles. It was a whole new experience for him. The way the story was reported in many circles was that the change was made because Magic asked to be traded, that because the team was 7–4 and had won five straight there were no sound basketball reasons for the change. He also knew that the fans might not treat him so kindly after reading some of the reports.

Dr. Buss continued to insist publicly that Magic had nothing to do with the firing. In fact, he said, he almost didn't fire Westhead precisely because of what Magic had said, because it would have looked as if Magic had caused the coaching change. But, he also said, if he hadn't fired Westhead despite Magic's statement, then he would have been allowing a player to affect a management decision.

Now Magic had to prepare for the fallout. He was told by friends to play right through the boos, to play winning basketball and all would soon be forgotten. The first game after the coaching change was against San Antonio at the Forum. When Magic's name was announced, a full house of 17,505 fans began to boo. As Magic said, "They booed long and hard." Magic stood there, literally fighting back the tears. For a split second, he might have been wishing he was back at Michigan State. He had been booed before as an opponent, but never by a home crowd and never for something that had happened off the court.

Maybe it was a combination of things including the huge contract. Multi-million dollar deals weren't nearly as commonplace in 1981 and fans stll had a hard time accepting and relating to them. Many asked how a player making a million dollars a year could complain about anything. By the end of the game, however, the Lakers began running the break, pulling away from the Spurs, and the boos abruptly turned to cheers.

But on the road it was different. Fans took the opportunity to give it to a guy who had beaten their team so many times already. In Seattle, some 20,000 fans booed nearly every time he touched the ball and they didn't stop until the game ended. By this time, Magic had been hearing the catcalls and boos for two straight weeks and on this night he said it affected his game. It was one of his worst of the year.

However, there were other things happening within the team, good things, signs that pointed to the return of the old Lakers, the running Lakers, the team that played Magic Johnson–type basketball. While Riley kept some of the set plays in the offense, he immediately returned the flexibility to the team. If the fast break was there, take it. He wanted the team to run, and basically turned them loose once again. He also re-established communication with his players. Not surprisingly, the team responded.

In late November and through December, the Lakers were again one of the hottest teams in the league. After Riley took over the coaching reins (Jerry West left the bench after a short time allowing Riley full control of the team) they won seventeen of twenty games, including a stretch of six straight while Kareem was out of the lineup with a bad ankle. Other teams just couldn't cope with the running game. Even one of the NBA's veteran refs kidded Magic about slowing the pace down, telling him the Lakers were going to run him out of the league.

When the team lost forward Mitch Kupchak to a severe knee injury, they signed former three-time scoring champion, Bob McAdoo, who had fallen on some hard times. But with the Lakers, McAdoo regained his scoring touch and became an important player. The problem was that after a hot December, the team had a cold January, playing .500 ball and making people wonder all over again if anything was wrong.

Magic wasn't voted to the All-Star team that year, being added by the coaches as a substitute. It was a further indication that his image and popularity had suffered, possibly because of his long-term contract, and definitely because of the way the Westhead firing was reported.

During the second half of the year the Lakers settled down. Time once again proved the great healer. Gradually, the turmoil of the early season was forgotten and the emphasis was again on basketball. Riley continued to allow the team to run, yet gained the respect of the players to the extent that if he wanted a set play or a half-court offense, no one carped. And, of course, it helped that they were winning.

When the season ended the Lakers were again atop the Pacific Division with a 57–25 record. Larry Bird and the Celtics had the best record in the league at 63–19. Maybe this time the two teams would finally meet for the championship. Whatever the result, it was increasingly obvious how much these two superstars had done for their teams and were doing for the NBA. They continued to be the two players the fans most wanted to see.

Magic had overcome the early-season turmoil to once again put together an all-star season. Playing in seventy-eight games, he averaged 18.6 points a game, had 751 rebounds and 743 assists, making him only the third player in league history (Wilt Chamberlain and Oscar Robertson were the others) to record more than 700 rebounds and 700 assists in the same year. He also led the league with 208 steals and set a club record with thirteen offensive rebounds in a game against Houston.

Now it was on to the playoffs and a chance for the Lakers to show everyone they were not only still a team, but still *the* team. In the conference semifinals, the Lakers had to deal with the Phoenix Suns, a very solid ballclub. No sweat. L.A. dispensed with the Suns in four straight games and moved into the Conference finals against the San Antonio Spurs. The Spurs were led by high-scoring guard George Gervin, who was one of Magic's early idols.

Gervin was the league's leading scorer that year and had solid support from forward Mike Mitchell. The Spurs were a high-scoring outfit that also liked to run and shoot. Maybe they could beat the Lakers at their own game. There was some concern about the Laker defense, which was just fifteenth in the league during the regular season. The offense was rated number two, and Riley hoped his defense could create enough turnovers and steals to really feed the running game. This would give Magic and Norm Nixon, with 1,395 assists between them, a chance to drive the Spurs to distraction with their dazzling passes.

"I hope we can disprove the theory that playoff basketball becomes a half-court game," he said. "I think teams go to the half-court game because they get too conservative."

Magic's biggest fear was that the Lakers would come in flat after a week off caused by the sweep of Phoenix. They had to wait for San Antonio to finish its series. "Sometimes a long layoff can cause a team to lose its rhythm," he said.

There was no need to worry. The Lakers came in razor-sharp and flying. The first game at the Forum was sometimes tantamount to a track meet, and while the Spurs weren't exactly the tortoise, the Lakers were definitely the hare. Riley's rabbits were off to the races with Magic running the show most of the time and

Nixon benefitting from his passing.

Nixon popped for thirty-one points, but that wasn't all. Kareem had thirty-two from in close and blocked five shots. A big lift came from McAdoo who scored twenty-one in a reserve role. The balanced attack offset Gervin's game high thirty-four and Mitchell's twenty-five. The Lakers won it, 128–117, and continued to streak toward the finals.

After the game, the Laker locker room was alive and kicking. The joking and jiving reverberated from every corner of the room. Winning can do that. This was the kind of camaraderie Magic loved. For him, it didn't get any better than being with a winning team that was doing it together. It was beginning to look as if the Lakers couldn't be stopped.

The Spurs refused to give an inch during the second game. They fought and scrapped, refusing to let the Lakers take control. When San Antonio got a 79–78 lead going into the final session, it looked as if they had a good chance to win. But the Lakers were like a time bomb waiting to explode. It happened when the Spurs missed ten of their first eleven shots in the final session. As soon as that happened, the Lakers began to run and they wound up with a 110–101 victory.

"It may not happen in the first period," Riley said, "or even in the second. But somewhere along the line the fast break is going to pay dividends. The other team is going to crack and we're going to have a spurt."

Riley had commanded more and more respect from the players as the season wore on. If he saw a weakness, he convinced the players to work on it. He seemed to have an instinct when it came to motivation. He could speak quietly but firmly, and he could occasionally explode. But there was no resentment. The players knew he wanted what was best for them, and in turn, what was best for the team.

On several occasions he even got on Magic about his defense, the one part of his game that needed work. It was no secret that he was not a great defensive player. Part of the reason might have been that his offensive responsibilities were always so diverse, hectic, and sometimes extremely tiring. If he had to cheat somewhere, it was on defense. Riley told him he needed more mental toughness, to decide ahead of time to shut his man down, then do it. He also told Magic that he had to be the team's spiritual leader, that he didn't have to holler, simply lead by example.

Now all the hard work was paying off. It was more of the same in the third game. Gervin had thirty-nine but it didn't matter; the Lakers played an opportunistic game, picking up loose balls and converting turnovers into breaks. They were making believers out of the San Antonio coaches.

"I don't know if any of the great Boston teams back in the '60s and '70s ever advanced the ball so quickly," Stan Albeck, the head coach, said. "We've tried everything in the book and we still couldn't stop them."

"They shoot more layups than any team that's ever played the game," added assistant coach Morris McHone.

It was more of the same in the fourth game. Gervin had thirty-eight and the Spurs battled all the way, but in the end the Lakers prevailed, 128–123, for yet another sweep. They were headed for the finals and were the first team to go 4–0 in consecutive series.

Again the basketball world was hoping for a Johnson–Bird, Laker–Celtic final. But once again the Philadelphia 76ers got in the way, upsetting the Celtics for the Eastern Conference title in seven games. So it would be a rematch of two years earlier, the Lakers and Sixers for the NBA title.

As for Magic, he was leaving the scoring to the likes

of Kareem, McAdoo, and Nixon. And his fellow guard noticed what he was doing.

"Magic is changing his game around," Norm Nixon said. "He's sacrificing his offense by going to the boards more and getting the ball out."

The roughest part of the sweep was again the long wait for the Eastern finals to end. But when L.A. finally got the Sixers on the court they looked as if they hadn't missed a beat. They won the opener, 124–117, for their ninth straight win of the playoffs. What was impressive was the way the Lakers came back from a 15–point deficit midway through the third period. It took that long to get things going. This time it was a half-court trap which led to the fast break and a 19–2 spurt that turned the game around.

Now the talk was of another sweep and a chance to really put the team in the history books. Riley told his ballclub to "go for it." Maybe they would have done it if the Sixers' Julius Erving, "Dr. J.," hadn't taken control of the second game. But then again, the Doctor was already considered an all-time great, and if anyone could turn a game around, he could. Leading an assault on the boards that resulted in the Sixers out-rebounding the Lakers, 52-39, the Doc inspired his teammates to a 110-94 victory

So the Laker winning streak was broken. Maybe it was a good thing. As Michael Cooper said, "This loss is to our benefit in a way. Now we just have to concentrate on being an NBA ballclub, not the greatest team of all time."

With the series moving to the Forum, the Lakers quickly gave their home fans a treat. They started running from the opening tap and never stopped. Magic and Jamaal Wilkes had nine points each in the first quarter as the Lakers jumped on top. Five times in the second period L.A. got the ball on the fast break and five times they scored. Twice the lead was twenty points before the half. It was "Showtime" at its best and Magic loved it.

"To me, it's the greatest high in basketball," he explained later. "There you are in the middle on the break, getting set to create something. It's almost like dancing to music and this is a boogie-woogie team. We might all have our own styles but as a team we dance real well."

This one was a laugher. The Lakers won it, 129–108, then took the fourth game, 111–101, and were just a game away from yet another title. Part of the success in games three and four was due to Magic playing head-up on the Doctor. He didn't keep him from getting on the scoreboard, but he used his body to keep Erving away from the boards. Doctor J had twenty-three rebounds in the first two games, but had just six in the next two, prompting Coach Riley to compliment his star.

"There isn't the excitement of [Magic's] rookie year," the coach said. "Then it was like going to Disneyland every day. Now he comes in and punches the clock like an old pro. But he's still our emotional catalyst. Everybody tunes into Magic and we struggle when he goes out of the game."

With his team on the brink of a championship, Magic talked about the strain caused by the early-season controversy.

"The toughest part has been keeping myself together mentally and concentrating," he said. "But all that stuff that happened really brought us together. We started hitting discos together and going to the movies in groups."

The team had to take some flak as a group in the fifth game. Kareem got in foul trouble early and Philly's Darryl Dawkins had one of his better outings. Plus the Lakers had eleven turnovers in the first quarter and never really got back on track. The Sixers won going away, 135–102, to pull within a game at 3–2.

Back at the Forum the Lakers sensed victory. Like the old Celtics, this was a team that just wouldn't lose two straight. There was some concern that morning when Kareem awoke with a terrible migraine headache. But once the game began, he quickly became a headache for the 76ers. The big guy was intimidating early on and not one of the Sixers' first four shots as much as touched the rim. In the meantime the Lakers ripped off a 9–0 lead and went on from there to win it, 114–104. They had defeated the 76ers in six games for the second time in three years to once again win the championship.

Wilkes led the way with twenty-seven points in the final game, but all the Lakers contributed. It was a real solid team victory. Though he was never mentioned as the team's leading scorer throughout the series, Magic Johnson was again named the Most Valuable Player of the finals. He did it with leadership, consistent play, and as one report said, "his new blue-collar work ethic."

The final game was typical of Magic's performance. He had thirteen points, thirteen rebounds, and thirteen assists, a neat and clean triple double. He also added four steals. He had to be happy about winning the title and the MVP once again. But perhaps the best thing that happened to him in a season in which he had run the emotional gamut was when a middle-aged woman caught his ear right after the game.

"I was one of the ones who booed you when Coach Westhead was fired," she said. "I just want you to know I'm sorry and I'll never boo you again."

CHAPTER

EIGHT

The Confrontation at Last

TWO CHAMPIONSHIPS IN THREE YEARS sandwiched between some pretty tough times—knee surgery, a controversial contract, and a fired coach—made Earvin Johnson acutely aware of the realities of professional sports. No matter how talented a player is, he can't always sit back and smell the roses. Rather, he has to keep his guard up. Get up too high atop that pedestal and someone will surely try to knock you off.

At the beginning of the 1982–83 season Magic was just twenty-three years old. Yet in some ways he probably felt he had already lived a lifetime in the NBA. He knew he had to stop worrying about how other people perceived him. As he had already learned, he wasn't always in control of his basketball destiny. A player, even a superstar, can be sabotaged both on and off the court.

Yet when a new season opens, it's a fresh start for everyone. Players have had a chance to rest from the arduous schedule, allowing their bodies to heal and to find renewed vigor for the beginning of a new training camp. It's even better when the player is returning to a team with the potential to do it again, to repeat as champions.

The Lakers surely had that chance. In fact, they even found themselves potentially stronger. Once again the Los Angeles team had parlayed a prior trade into the number-one pick in the entire draft. It was the first time a reigning champion had first choice and the team used it well. They tapped James Worthy, a 6'9", All American forward out of the University of North Carolina. Worthy had helped the Tar Heels to a national championship the year before and had been named the Most Valuable Player of the Final Four, having scored twenty-eight points in the title game against Georgetown. He was considered about as close to a "can't miss" prospect as you could get.

Opening night at the Forum, the team held a ceremony in which the championship rings from the previous year were given out. Ironically, the defending champs then lost to the Golden State Warriors, 132–117. But there was nothing to worry about. From there the team went into high gear immediately, winning their next seven games with the same kind of alert, fast break basketball that had characterized their run to the title the season before.

If there was any concern on the ballclub it was the age of the big guy. Kareem Abdul-Jabbar was thirty-five years old at the outset of the season and beginning his fourteenth NBA campaign. It was already a long and glorious career and there were those wondering just how much more he had left, especially playing center for a running, fast breaking team. But Kareem always kept himself in top condition, rarely missed a game, and looked to be ready for another outstanding year.

The script went pretty much according to plan. L.A. had another fine season, to finish at 58–24 and take the Pacific Division title once more. Toward the end of the year, however, there were a couple of signs that fate was working against them. Bob McAdoo, who had become a vital part of the Laker machine, missed the final thirty-two games of the season with a toe injury. Then, just before the playoffs were due to begin, rookie Worthy suffered a broken leg and was gone. Worthy had been putting together a fine rookie season to that point.

As for Magic, it had been yet another fine year. He was named to the all-NBA first team for the first time after leading the league in assists. He averaged 10.5 assists per game and his total of 829 broke Jerry West's club record. His scoring average was down to 16.8, but only because he was distributing the ball so often.

In the playoffs, the Lakers handled the Portland Trailblazers with relative ease, winning in five games. Kareem had a great series, playing forty minutes a game, averaging over thirty points and blocking more than five shots each time out. It was hard to believe he was now thirty-six.

"When you start making concessions to age, age will take over," he said, succinctly.

Yet as the Lakers went up against San Antonio for the Western Conference title, Pat Riley was worried. It was the injury to Worthy that he felt had really hurt, especially after McAdoo was lost.

"James' injury had a big effect on the team psychologically," the coach said. "It was disruptive because the other guys suddenly had to play more minutes and play different positions. Our whole substitution rotation had to change."

Yet the team still managed to top San Antonio in six games and now had a good chance to repeat as champions. Once again the Philadelphia 76ers were the Lakers' opponents, but with one major change. Moses Malone had joined the Sixers as their center and had made a good team great. The Sixers finally broke through and did it in fine style. They shocked everyone by whipping the Lakers in four straight to become the new champs.

Maybe it was the playoff loss, maybe just a decision to shake up the team, but prior to the 1983–84 season there was a major trade. The team sent Norm Nixon, guard Eddie Jordan, and a pair of draft choices to San Diego in exchange for rookie guard Byron Scott and veteran center Swen Nater. The key figures in the deal were Nixon and Scott. Scott was a pure shooting guard and by trading Nixon, the Lakers were telling Magic that he could finally have complete control of the backcourt. Though he and Nixon managed to work well together, having two point guards in the same backcourt was still sometimes awkward. Now Magic could handle the ball all the time.

Now the pieces were in place for two very memorable seasons. They weren't necessarily memorable because the Lakers won another pair of Pacific Division titles. That was becoming old hat. And they weren't memorable because of the continued fine play of Kareem Abdul-Jabbar, the march to stardom of James Worthy, or the continued crowd-pleasing performance of Magic Johnson. No, the 1983–84 and 1984–85 seasons would be memorable because they would both conclude with the confrontation basketball fans had been waiting for since 1979–80.

It was a great rivalry even before they came, but now the NBA's showcase championship series would feature its two most exciting young players. In both years the Lakers would finally be clashing with the Boston Celtics for the NBA championship. And that would mean the resumption of the personal rivalry between Magic Johnson and Larry Bird.

In 1983–84, the Lakers finished at 54–28, four games off the pace of a year earlier. Magic, however, dislocated a finger on December 2, and missed about a month of action. That didn't help. He returned, however, in time to set an NBA All-Star Game record by passing off for twenty-two assists, many of them to Kareem, who scored twenty-five points and hauled down thirteen rebounds. The big guy seemed to be getting better with age.

In April, Kareem reached another milestone by breaking Wilt Chamberlain's all-time NBA scoring record. On the downside, Jamaal Wilkes suffered an intestinal infection in February and never really regained his top form for the rest of the season. But the team still won as Magic had a career-best 875 assists.

The Celtics topped their division with a 62–20 record, as Bird had a career best 24.2 scoring average. But, like Magic, it was all the other avenues he provided that made him great. And the Celtics, like the Lakers, were far from a one-man team. Bird had the kind of support in Boston that he never had at Indiana State.

Center Robert Parish and forward Kevin McHale joined Bird to form one of the best front lines in basketball. Dennis Johnson was perhaps the toughest defensive guard in the league, a player fully capable of giving Magic fits. Danny Ainge could light it up from long range, as could Scott Wedman. Veteran Cedric Maxwell was still a fine player, while another pair of vets, Quinn Buckner and M.L. Carr provided savvy and relief. The Celts were a very sound team, with that great Boston winning tradition to motivate them and

Larry Bird to lead them.

Both teams rolled through the playoffs to win conference titles and the confrontation everyone wanted was finally a reality. Even though the two superstars were both great team players and wanted to avoid direct comparisons, everyone knew all eyes would be on their every move.

"You can't blame them for feeling that way," said former college coach Pete Newell, who was then a consultant with the Golden State Warriors. "But these are two of the greatest players we've ever had. Magic may be a guard and Larry a forward, but you know people are going to compare them. I know both of them will want to be at their best."

"It's like the opening of a great play," said Jerry West. "Everybody is waiting to see it."

Maybe it wasn't fair to the other great players on both teams, but people wouldn't stop talking about Johnson and Bird. There were stories about other great personal rivalries and comparisons, such as the Bill Russell–Wilt Chamberlain rivalry when the two great centers of the 1960s went up against each other. Then there was West and his rivalry with Oscar Robertson when they were the two best guards in the game and at that time maybe the best ever.

Now there was Johnson and Bird, and many people felt these two players had already taken the game to another dimension. One writer even said that the great Julius Erving couldn't compare with them.

"Erving was never the player Bird or Magic is," he wrote. "He's a conventional forward with extraordinary physical abilities. But if you're talking about the greatest all-around player in the game, you've got to be talking about Bird or Magic."

Jerry West, who had watched Magic close up with the Lakers from the beginning, also loved Bird's game.

"He whets your appetite for the game," West said of the Celtic forward. "He's such a great passer and he doesn't make mistakes. Magic handles the ball more, so he makes more mistakes. Larry Bird is a genius on the basketball floor."

The debate as to which one was better could go on and on. It was really just a matter of preference and style. What was certain, however, was the mutual admiration society between the two stars.

Magic talked about the similar qualities the two had.

"Me and Larry are just different from everybody else," he said. "It's not like we're just two great scorers, because you can shut scorers down. We do so many other things. Even if one of us isn't scoring, we make our presence felt." Then he added, "He's definitely the best player at this time."

Bird talked about the differences.

"We both do the same things, but we're not the same type player," he said. "The impact I have on a game is usually scoring, but with him it's always his passing. He has his hands on the ball more than I do, so he has more control of the situation. So you can't really compare us . . . Magic is just beyond description. I think of him as one of the three top players in the game today, maybe the best. He's a perfect player."

And before it all started, Magic smiled at a reporter who asked a similar question for the umpteenth time. All Magic said was: "Me and Larry at last."

The series opened in the ancient Boston Garden with its distinctive parquet floor. Fans couldn't help notice all the championship banners hanging conspicuously from the rafters. There were eleven from the Russell–Cousy years, another pair from the '70s when John Havlicek and Dave Cowens led the team, and the most recent from 1980–81, thanks to Larry Bird and company. Joining the championship banners were the symbolic jerseys of the retired stars—Russell, Cousey, Havlicek, Cowens, Tom Heinsohn, Bill Sharman, Frank Ramsey, Sam and K.C. Jones, among others—serving as a constant reminder of Celtic pride and Celtic tradition. The Celtics were the New York Yankees of basketball and Boston was extremely tough to beat in their old, creaky building.

But the Lakers showed their disrepect for that tradition early. They came out running and raced to a 24–9 lead before the Celtics could get it together. Kareem hit his first six shots, serving notice that at age thirty-seven he was still considerably more than window dressing. And Magic ran the offense with confidence, flashing his smile from time to time and whipping his accurate passes all over the court. With Magic leading the way, the Lakers got eleven fast break points in the first period alone.

Another mismatch saw 6'2" Celtic guard Gerald Henderson trying to stay with Magic. The size difference was too great, giving the Laker star a big advantage. At the same time, the 6'7" Michael Cooper put the clamps somewhat on Bird. Always a tenacious defender, the willowy Cooper held Bird to just ten points in the first half.

Bird came alive somewhat in the second half, leading a Boston comeback that brought the score to 105–101 with 5:05 left. But the Lakers never lost their poise and went on to win it, 115–109. To defeat the Celtics at the Boston Garden in game one was a real feat and made L.A. heavy favorites to take the series.

Magic had played very well, scoring eighteen points, handing out ten assists, and grabbing six rebounds. Bird had twenty-four points, but hit just seven of seventeen from the field. He had fourteen boards and five assists. It was Kareem, however, who led all the scorers with thirty-two. But the bottom line was the Lakers had a 1–0 lead in games and if they could take the second game, they would be in great shape to win yet another title.

The Celtics knew they had to adjust to the Laker break, which produced fifty-two points in the opening game. It helped in the second game that their outside shooting came alive. That's one way to equalize the break—hit your shots. Boston scored the first seven points and took a 36–26 first quarter lead. It would have been a bigger lead had not Magic scored fourteen early points. Then, when the Lakers got their running game going in the second quarter, they chipped away at the lead which was down to 61–59 at the half.

Midway through the third period the Celts again led by seven, but James Worthy got the hot hand and scored eleven of his team's next twelve points. In the fourth period it began to look as if it would go down to the wire. With just 1:12 left, a three-point play by Worthy tied the game 111–111. Then with thirty-five seconds remaining, Magic was fouled. He calmly sank both free throws to give his team a two-point lead at 113–111.

Now it was crunch time. Boston's Kevin McHale missed two foul shots at the twenty-second mark and it appeared to be over. But the Celtics pressed, forcing Magic to pass to Worthy, then denying him a return pass. Worthy's pass was picked off by Henderson who raced down court to score the tying basket with thirteen seconds on the clock. The Lakers tried to isolate Magic and Kareem on the left side, hoping one of them could get a shot. Magic dribbled around for ten seconds looking for the pass, couldn't make it, and time ran out. The game went to overtime.

The Lakers took a quick lead again, but Boston

wouldn't quit. Finally, a Scott Wedman jumper gave Boston a 122–121 advantage with fourteen seconds left. Once again the Lakers couldn't get a shot off. Parish stole a Wilkes pass to stop one attempt, then seconds later he knocked the ball away from McAdoo. Bird's two free throws capped the 124–121 victory.

Back in L.A. for game three, the Lakers rolled. This one wasn't even close. With Magic handing out a championship-series record twenty-one assists, the Lakers ran to a 137–104 victory.

"It was everybody," said Magic. "It feels so good when it happens so fast that way. There's just nothing a defense can do about it."

Game four was a key. If the Lakers won they would have an almost insurmountable, 3–1, lead. M.L. Carr, a veteran player with the Celts, felt his team let it get away by playing too soft.

"It's probably too late now," said Carr, "but what we should have done right from the start was set Worthy or Magic or someone on his can and then we should have done it again. Then they would have known we meant business and maybe they wouldn't have been so fearless going inside."

Carr's war cry didn't go unheeded. Midway through the third quarter of the fourth game the Lakers held a 76–70 lead. That's when Boston's Kevin McHale clotheslined L.A.'s Kurt Rambis under the hoop while Rambis was going in for what appeared to be an uncontested layup. Both benches emptied. Minutes later, Kareem threw an elbow at Bird and the two stars began jawing at each other. After that, the flow of the game changed. It was Celtic basketball, a rough-and-tumble game that resembled the style of play of the 1950s. As Magic said: "Those incidents definitely helped them and hurt us. Now we know that if they have to elbow, smack us, or slam us to win, they'll do it."

Yet with fifty-six seconds left, a pair of free throws by Magic made it a 113–108 game. It looked like another L.A. win. But then Robert Parish converted a three-point play and three seconds later Kareem fouled Bird and at the same time fouled out of the game. Bird made another pair of free throws and the game was tied.

With sixteen seconds left, the Lakers again looked for a last shot and a win. Magic dribbled about ten seconds off the clock, then tried to lob a pass to Worthy. The pass was tipped and then intercepted by Parish. Luckily, both Bird and McHale missed last-second shots and the game went into overtime.

Again both teams battled it out. With thirty-five seconds left the game was tied at 123. Magic was fouled and had a pair of free throws to give his team the lead. Incredibly, he missed both. Bird then hit the clutch shot and the pugnacious Carr stole the Lakers' final in-bounds pass and dunked, giving the Celtics a 129–125 win and tying the series at two games each. In the minds of many, the Lakers had let an opportunity slip away.

It was back to Boston for game five. The Boston Garden had no air conditioning then and the heat was oppressive, approaching 100 degrees on the court. In fact, one of the refs became so dehydrated that he collapsed, and at halftime the Celtic players showered and changed uniforms. Whether it was the heat or the stingy Boston defense, the Lakers couldn't get it going. They had only fifteen fast break points and shot under 43 percent from the floor.

Bird, who had scored twenty-nine points and pulled down twenty-one rebounds in the fourth game, was hot again. He blistered the Lakers for thirty-four points on fifteen for twenty shooting as the Celtics won big, 121–103. Now, it was the Lakers whose backs were up against the wall. After the game, Kareem talked about the heat.

"It was like taking a sauna with all your clothes on, then doing 100 pushups before running up and down the court for 48 minutes."

Magic didn't have a good game either. He was seeing more of Dennis Johnson on defense, and while only 6'4", D.J. was one of the best defensive guards in the game. He kept muscling Magic away from the center of the court, thereby limiting his effectiveness. So it was the Lakers who had to regroup for game six or say sayonara.

For most of the afternoon, even the Great Western Forum didn't look too friendly. Kareem had one of his migraine headaches and the Celtics were giving the Lakers another. They led most of the way and with five minutes left in the third quarter it was an 84–73 game. It looked even worse when Magic had to come out of the game to rest an aching right knee.

That's when L.A. got an unexpected lift. Rookie Byron Scott and James Worthy sparked a rally that enabled L.A. to tie the game at 93 with 6:41 left to play. By then, Magic was back and the running game was moving into high gear. Kareem's headache was gone and the big guy was contributing a big second half. When it ended the Lakers had a 119-108 victory and had tied the series at three games each. Now it was back to Boston for the seventh and deciding contest. For both fans and the league itself, the scenario couldn't have been better.

Kareem had again showed his true grit with a thirty-point, ten-rebound performance in forty-two minutes of action in the sixth game.

"His effort meant so much to us," said Magic. "When your leader has strength like that, you have to follow him."

Even the usually laid-back center was psyched. "You hear a lot about Celtic pride and tradition," Kareem said, "but we've got some of that here, too. There was never any question that I was going to play."

So the classic confrontation came down to one game. The Celtics had their strategy set. Keep the ball down low and hit the offensive boards as hard as they could. If they made it difficult for the Lakers to rebound, the L.A. couldn't get its feared fast break in gear. The strategy worked.

The Celtics were outmuscling the Lakers underneath almost from the opening tap. Even Pat Riley acknowledged that this type of game could beat his team.

"Our club is wiry and footloose," he said. "But an aggressive team that rebounds will win because it will create more opportunities for inside play and free throws."

The continuing defensive job that Dennis Johnson was doing on Magic was also a factor. In addition, the tendonitis in Magic's left knee slowed him somewhat, and the physical play by D.J. made it worse. Some said Magic appeared fatigued in the second half. The Celtic defense, especially D.J.'s, also caused the Lakers and Magic to use too much of the twenty-four-second clock and caused them to hurry their half-court offense. Perhaps the most graphic description of what was happening came from Celtic Cedric Maxwell.

"Before, the Lakers were just running across the street whenever they wanted," Maxwell said. "Now, they stop at the corner, push the button, wait for the light, and look both ways."

In the end, Boston's 52–33 edge in rebounding was the difference. The Celts had a 58–52 lead at the half, then showed their power in the third quarter when they increased it to 91–78. The Laker fast break just wasn't there. The final was 111–102, and still another championship banner would be hoisted in the Boston

Garden. In fact, the seventh-game victory would have been even more one-sided had the Celts not shot just 39.5 percent from the field. That made their win even more remarkable.

Not surprisingly, Bird was the MVP, having averaged 27.4 points and fourteen rebounds a game. Magic averaged eighteen points and set a record with ninety-five assists. But he also committed thirty-one turnovers and definitely came out second best in the ultimate confrontation.

"I've gained a greater appreciation for Larry in this series because it seemed he did more for our success than Magic did for theirs," said one Celtic team official. "Magic was great, but only when the Lakers were ahead."

No one denied the Boston domination. Kareem admitted that "the best team won. If you can't make it happen on the court, you don't deserve it."

In the eyes of many, the biggest loser was Earvin Johnson. It was the first time he and Bird had a prolonged clash in the pros and it seemed that he showed some weaknesses in his game. While the criticism probably hurt, Magic tried to stay positive.

"This series was special," he said. "It's what you live for. I'd rather play in the finals four times and lose, than not be in them at all. I'm two and two now, but I can say that I was here."

Other than the Celtics, the big winner was the NBA. The final game attracted the largest TV audience in NBA history and some will point to the entire final round as the point in which the league began the popular and financial rebirth that would make it a booming business and rousing success story by the end of the decade. And again, the two principals most responsible for the resurgence were Earvin Johnson and Larry Bird.

Unfortunately, Magic had taken a bit of a beating in

the reputation department. Critics pointed out that at the conclusion of games two, four, and seven when a big play was needed, Magic didn't come through. It happens to everyone, but when it's crunch time in the finals on center stage, everyone is there to see it.

It would not be an easy series to forget. Both Magic and Michael Cooper stayed in the showers so long after the seventh game that someone had to go look for them. They were just sitting there, letting the water cascade off them and talking about the series just concluded. Magic couldn't sleep the whole night. He just sat in his Boston hotel room talking some more, this time with two of his closest friends, Isiah Thomas and Mark Aguirre. None of them slept until morning.

Not one to alibi, Magic admitted to his mistakes long after they happened. "We made five mistakes that cost us the series," he said, "and I contributed to three of them."

Even Larry Bird had said, upon reflection, that "the Lakers should have swept us in four games."

So the onus was on Magic. Until the loss to the Celtics, everything in his life seemed to be falling into place. He had built a beautiful new mansion in Bel Air, California, had a huge salary, and very lucrative endorsement and business dealings. Yet as he had said so often, it was basketball that meant the most to him. When you lost the big game, everything else seemed trivial, at least back then. There were constant reminders of the series, reminders that he had shot just five for fourteen from the floor in the final game and had committed seven turnovers. He couldn't stop thinking about it all summer.

"I'll be sitting somewhere just relaxing," he said, "and suddenly it's all there in my mind. I can still see Worthy open."

It was not a pleasant offseason. A headline in the Los Angeles Times asked, EARVIN, WHAT HAPPENED TO MAGIC? He was called the goat of the series, "Tragic" Johnson, and "the tarnished superstar." Another story said that with the entire world watching him and "right there against his arch-rival, Larry Bird, he failed."

His mother commented that he didn't smile as much now, that there was a new look of determination on his face. Coach Riley explained that Magic was extremely sensitive about what people thought of him.

"The wounds from last June stayed open all summer," Riley said. "He feels he has to concentrate more and I think the whole experience has made him grow up in a lot of ways."

Someone pointed out that ever since his remarkable performance in the sixth game of the championship series his rookie year, all the bad things that have happened with the Lakers have somehow been turned toward him.

"It's going to fall on somebody's shoulders," Magic said, philosophically. "It just always seems to come back to mine, one way or another."

There were stories all over again about how the booing affected him after he was blamed for the Westhead firing. Pat Riley, who was Westhead's assistant, could only reiterate that the entire situation wasn't Magic's fault.

"Magic just heard the mutinous attitude among the players and wondered how long it could go on," said Riley. "I think what he said about wanting to be traded was a cry for help, but for the whole team. He acted as a spokesman, that's all. I think there was a lot of pressure put on him by his teammates to say something."

Seeing what was happening, some rushed to Magic's defense. Denver coach Doug Moe credited Magic with rejuvenating and prolonging the career of Abdul-Jabbar.

"At one point I thought Kareem had had it with basketball," said Moe. "He loafed a lot, but he plays harder now than he did before Magic was there."

And the big guy himself said that Magic's playing personality was nowhere near being egotistic.

"All he wants to do is get the ball to somebody else and let them score," Kareem said. "And if you're a big man, it's not hard to like somebody like that."

But perhaps it was Pat Riley who put the whole thing in perspective. "People say he has to come back now and prove himself all over again," said Riley. "That's a joke."

The Lakers opened the 1984–85 season with basically the same cast of characters. They quickly showed they were again one of the best teams in the league, utilizing their fast break and working to improve on their half-court game at the same time. Kareem continued to play well and in December announced he would be back for an unprecedented seventeenth season in 1985–86. Magic also seemed to suffer no ill effects to his game. In fact, his popularity was still enormous. It was proven in mid-season when he received a record 957,447 votes in the All-Star balloting.

In the second half of the season the injury jinx hit the team again. Jamaal Wilkes tore up a knee in February and wouldn't return. He had been a key member of the ballclub right through the '80s. Despite his loss, the team finished strongly. They won thirty-one of their final thirty-five games, including seventeen in a row at home. In March, they were 13–1 and finished the year at 62–20, Pacific Division champs by a record twenty games.

Magic had a typical year, with an 18.3 average and career best 968 assists. But as soon as the season ended, he and his teammates looked to the playoffs. There were the Celtics again, atop their division at

63–19. That was the team the Lakers wanted, a rematch with Boston, another confrontation of the league's reigning superstars. Magic wanted it, too. He wanted a chance to erase the playoff pain of a year earlier.

Now everyone could focus on the playoffs. During the season, however, there had been a slight diversion, but one that would ultimately be great for the NBA. The Chicago Bulls had unveiled a rookie from North Carolina named Michael Jordan. Jordan was spectacular from day one, exciting the fans with aerial acrobatics and mid-air contortions that left opponents shaking their heads in disbelief. He averaged 28.2 points a game as a rookie and would become the most exciting offensive player of his time. Combined with Magic and Larry Bird, "Air" Jordan would become the third of a triumvirate of popular superstars who would continue to help the league grow and prosper, putting its tarnished image of a few years earlier out to pasture for good.

The playoffs went according to schedule. The Lakers eliminated the Phoenix Suns in three straight games, then the Portland Trailblazers and Denver Nuggets in five games to reach the championship round. In the East, Boston dumped the Cleveland Cavaliers in four, then took the Detroit Pistons in six and the Philadelphia 76ers in five games. It was perfect. The rematch was about to happen, classic confrontation number two.

CHAPTER NINE

A Winner Once More

I T MUST HAVE SEEMED LIKE A BAD CASE OF
deja vu when the Lakers traveled to the
Boston Garden for game one of their
championship series and got their heads handed to
them on a Celtic platter. The score tells the story—
Boston 148, Los Angeles 114. And when someone asked
why the Lakers didn't have many rebounds, Kareem
answered: "When you're always pulling the ball out of
the net, there are no rebounds and you can't run."

The Celtics were unconscious. They shot 60.8 percent for the game, many of the shots of the long-range
variety. Even Celtics coach K.C. Jones couldn't believe it.

"It was one of those days where, if you turn around
and close your eyes, the ball is going to go in."

Boston demonstrated it all afternoon. Reserve guard

Scott Wedman was totally on fire, hitting on all eleven of his shots, including four from three-point range. The outcome of the game was never in doubt. While it was obvious that the Celtics couldn't shoot that way every night, there was a chance that such a huge victory in the first game could demoralize the Lakers, who still had painful memories of a year earlier. That's why game two, also at Boston, was so vital. If the Celtics could blow Los Angeles out a second straight time, the series would probably be over.

One thing the Lakers vowed to do was play the Celtics' game. Riley lit into his team and promised fines for sloppy rebounding and lazy defense. Bob McAdoo reminded his teammates where they were and what they had to do.

"You don't get to the finals without rebounding and hitting people," he said.

So the Lakers went to work. Riley used his bench more and the team wasn't delicate about committing fouls. On defense, the Lakers were playing it tough and very aggressive. They were contending for every loose ball and making sure they took the Celtics out of their shooting rhythm, especially from the outside.

The game was rough from start to finish. This time the Lakers didn't back down. Assistant Coach Dave Wohl said Boston "expected us to crawl into a hole. It's like the bully on the block who keeps taking your lunch money every day. Finally, you get tired of it, and you whack him."

One target was Celts forward Kevin McHale. He had ignited his team when he clotheslined Kurt Rambis on a fast break the year before. This year, McHale had been in a verbal war with Coach Riley, referring to the Celtics as "longshoremen" and the Lakers as "movie stars." Even with the Lakers' new philosophy, the series didn't turn until late in the second quarter of the second game. Boston still had a 48–38 lead when the Lakers suddenly went on a 10–1 run to pull within one, then added another burst before the buzzer to take a 65–59 lead into the locker room.

Boston made a run in the third period before Kareem took over. With Magic pounding the ball inside to the big guy, Abdul-Jabbar began hitting the sky hook. He might have been thirty-eight years old, but the sky hook looked as if it would go on forever. Along the way, he became the league's all-time playoff scorer, but later shook off questions about the record.

"The record was not the thing I was after," he said.

He was after a victory and got it as the Lakers won the game, 109–102, to even the series at a game apiece. Now both clubs flew to Los Angeles for the third game. Their confidence bolstered, the Lakers vowed to continue to match the Celtics physically.

Unlike the series a year earlier, Larry Bird was not shooting well. He was well under fifty percent in games two and three. In the third game the Lakers began to run and whenever that happened, the older, slower Celtics had trouble keeping up. And when they weren't running, Magic and company were mixing it up with the Beantowners. Bird and Rambis landed in a heap and Boston's Danny Ainge promptly jumped into the fray, prompting Bird to say later: "We should meet them out in the parking lot and have a fight to get it out of our system. I don't know if the league is up for it, but the Celtics are."

There was obviously no love lost between the two ballclubs. Later in the game, Magic got into a shoving match with McHale, then McAdoo and the tall Celtic forward got into it. Abdul-Jabbar couldn't contain a small grin when he said, "We're not out to hurt them, but I wouldn't mind hurting their feelings."

They must have hurt some feelings in game three, to

the tune of an easy, 136–111 victory. It was almost pay-
back for the Boston blowout in game one. Now came
the pivotal fourth game. Another win and the Lakers
would be on the brink of a title.

But the flow and ebb of the series—and of the rivalry
—continued in game four, with a little help from the
league office and some sly work by Celtics' coach K.C.
Jones. Before the game, the NBA's vice-president of
operations, Scotty Stirling, had informed both coaches
that the rough stuff wouldn't be tolerated. If it occurred
again, fines would be in order. Pat Riley informed his
club of the warning, but K.C. Jones figured that some
things were better left unsaid.

Whether the Lakers held back or not was difficult to
say, but they looked a bit flat and the game stayed
close. When they did take a slim lead, they couldn't
hold it. Finally it came down to one last shot. Bird got
the ball to Dennis Johnson and D.J. canned a twenty-
one-foot jumper to win it for Boston, 107–105. So the
Celtics had won another close one, causing Michael
Cooper to question the character of his team.

"It makes you wonder when they win all the games
decided by one or two points," said Coop. "Those are
the games where you see the heart of a good ball team.
We've just got to buckle down and win one of these."

The 1984–85 playoffs was the first year the home
court format had changed. Up until then it was two
games at one court, two at the other, then the teams
would alternate one game on each court for the final
three. Now it was like baseball's World Series, two
games at one site, three at the other, then the last two
at the first site again. So game five would be the last at
Los Angeles. Even if the Lakers won it, they would still
have to clinch at Boston. If they lost, forget it.

Fortunately, the Lakers rediscovered their aggres-
siveness in game five. Riley pulled a successful maneu-

ver by taking Kareem off Robert Parish and switching him over to McHale, who was having a brilliant series. Never a tenacious defender in the Bill Russell or Wilt Chamberlain mold, Kareem nevertheless managed to keep McHale away from the boards and that was the most important thing.

The Lakers were also helping out. When McHale launched a short jumper from the lane, Worthy came flying from the side and blocked it. Rambis then dove into the courtside seats to keep the ball in play. Then, just before the half, the Lakers put on one of their typical spurts, going on a 14–3 run to take a 64–51 lead into the locker room.

In the third period it was the Celtics' turn. That was the interesting thing about these rivals. Each team seemed to always make a run at the other, just when a game seemed out of reach. This time the Lakers had an 89–72 advantage, but the Celts trimmed it to 101–97 with 6:01 left. It was again anyone's game. Then the Lakers' two main men took over.

During the next several minutes, Magic tossed in three baskets and Kareem added a trio of sky hooks, followed by a a slam dunk. That did it. The final score was 120–111. Even though they were going back to Boston for the sixth game, the Lakers felt they were in control.

"People didn't think we could win the close games," said Magic. "But we won one tonight." He also felt the Celtics were tiring out. "They have only been playing seven guys. Kareem and me hadn't played much because of foul trouble, and we were running off the long jumpers they were taking."

Those long jumpers weren't falling, not nearly the way they had in the first game, and when game six began, the Lakers were looking for more of the same. Pat Riley said his team would be ready.

"We're not going to be careful," Riley said. "We're going to be *carefree*. If they thought we ran last night, they're going to see us run some more. Sometime in the course of the game, one team is going to crack. And if we push it, it's more likely to be them."

Boston had never lost the final game of a championship series at home but Abdul-Jabbar, for one, saw it happening this time.

"It's like the old Brooklyn Dodgers beating the Yankees back in 1955," he said, invoking his New York roots. "It wasn't supposed to happen, but it did. Celtic pride is supposed to be in this building, but so are we."

From the opening tap the Lakers applied the pressure. Magic was running the ball up court every chance he had. And during each time-out, Riley told his team not to let up for a second.

"I could see they were tired all over their faces," said Magic. "Riles kept making that point, telling me to keep pushing it. Even if we pushed it up and didn't score, my job was still to push it. To keep pushing it till they broke."

The Celtics tried to rely on their outside shooting again, but fatigue can sabotage long jump shots. The legs go first and when a shooter can't jump quite the same way, he loses the rhythm of his shot. The Celts were again shooting less than forty percent. Only Kevin McHale was having a big game, while Bird was also scoring, but missing too many shots. On the Laker side, Magic was content to feed both Worthy and Abdul-Jabbar, who were each playing extremely well.

When Kareem had to go to the bench with foul trouble, Riley went to Mitch Kupchak, who was making a comeback after very serious knee surgery. Kupchak played a physical, aggressive game against McHale and kept up just where the big guy left off. While the Lakers never completely blew the Celtics out, they kept the lead the entire game and wound up with a 111–100 victory. They had done it. They had won the championship and had finally beaten the Celtics.

"We made them lose it," crowed a happy Magic, after it was over.

For the Lakers, Abdul-Jabbar was a unanimous choice for Most Valuable Player, scoring eighteen of his twenty-nine points in the second half. Young James Worthy played one his greatest games ever, finishing with twenty-eight points in the clincher. Bird, the MVP during the regular season, had twenty-eight but only on twelve-for-twenty-nine shooting. Magic averaged 17.5 points during the nineteen total games in the post season, adding 289 assists and 134 rebounds. After it was over, he couldn't contain his enthusiasm for the play of the big guy.

"Kareem amazes me," Magic said. "But then again he doesn't. He's just Kareem and he was focusing in. Nobody and nothing stops him once his back hits the wall."

As for Magic, he was asked point-blank how he felt after beating the Celtics, especially after the disappointing playoffs of a year earlier. Once again he flashed that mile-wide smile and said, emphatically: "I'm back. *Back!*"

CHAPTER TEN

A Young Elder Statesman

IN A SENSE, THE VICTORY OVER THE CELTICS brought the first pnase of Magic Johnson's career full cycle. It was the third time he had played on a championship team, yet he needed the win over Bird and the Celtics very badly. It really shouldn't have been that way, but it was. Public perception changes rapidly and after the loss to the Celts in 1983–84, a great deal of his early success seemed forgotten. People appeared to remember the controversy and those few, fundamental blown plays in the championship round.

That's because it's not easy being a hero, especially in the sports world. *What have you done for me lately?* is, unfortunately, often the prevailing mentality when it comes to sports figures, especially those who have had success early. Magic was a champion his final year in college and a champion again his first year as a pro. Because of that, the public perception was that he should be a champion every year. Lose a few and you get no sympathy. It's the old story. People prefer to root for the underdog. To root for a hero, he has to stay on top. Otherwise . . .

When Wilt Chamberlain was at the peak of his career he was often booed by fans, despite once averaging fifty points a game for an entire season. At 7'1" and 275 pounds, he often looked like a man playing against boys, such was his physical advantage. It wasn't until Chamberlain's final years, when a young Lew Alcindor (Kareem Abdul-Jabbar) came into the league to challenge him, that Wilt was finally cheered. He had a favorite saying for that. *Nobody loves Goliath!* Wilt would repeat that on more than one occasion.

To the public, Magic Johnson was almost a Goliath in those early years. And when a few cracks in the armor appeared—whether it be his involvement in Laker politics, or his play on the hardwood—people were quick to exclaim that he wasn't quite what they thought. Larry Bird had been the regular season Most Valuable Player in the NBA in both 1984 and '85. Magic had still not won that coveted prize. But as the 1985–86 season approached, things would slowly equalize. Magic was just twenty-six years old at the start of the new campaign, but it somehow seemed he had been around a lot longer than that.

The nucleus of the team was back once again. A young forward named A.C. Green would begin to make his presence felt, eventually replacing Rambis. But the essence of the team was still Magic, Byron Scott, Worthy, and Kareem. This was a ballclub that had reached the championship round four straight years. And the way they started the new season, it looked as if it would be five.

Los Angeles came out of the gate as if they were on automatic pilot. The team got off to the best start in its history, winning 11 of its first twelve games, ninteen of its first twenty-one and twenty-four of its first twenty-seven. With a 24–3 record there wasn't much anyone could say that was less than glowing. The club was playing with a thirty-seven-year-old center who seemed to have found the fountain of youth. Kareem had forty points in an early-season game against the New York Knicks and their center, Patrick Ewing. Then he came back and got forty-six against Houston and Akeem (now Hakeem) Olajuwon. Ewing and Olajuwon were considered the two top young centers in the game. Kareem's forty-six-point explosion was his largest output since 1975.

All the other Lakers were contributing as well. Worthy had become a bona fide star, while Scott was a fine shooter at off guard and a solid defender. Michael Cooper was arguably the best defensive player in the league and a super sub. As for Magic, he was again leading the NBA in assists and playing well. In addition, the smile was back on his face. When it was time for the All-Star balloting, the Lakers were way out in front of the Pacific Division and Magic became the first player ever to get more than one million votes. He was joined by Abdul-Jabbar and Worthy in the West's starting lineup. The Lakers seemed to be *the* team.

Though Los Angeles slowed its pace somewhat in the second half, it was almost understandable. They were cruising to a sixth straight Pacific Division title with no one to challenge them. They wound up 62–20 for the second year in a row and set another NBA record by winning their division by a full twenty-two games.

Magic had an outstanding year, averaging 18.8 points a game and winning his third assist title with 907. But once again both he and his teammates saw their regular-season thunder stolen by the Celtics. Boston had an NBA best record of 67–15 and Larry Bird would be awarded his third consecutive Most Valuable Player prize. At this point in their careers, Bird's individual achievements had exceeded Magic's, though that doesn't necessary mean one is better than the other.

Once again, NBA publicists rubbed their hands together at the prospect of another Celtics–Lakers meeting in the finals. Both clubs were odds-on favorites to capture their conference titles. But things don't always work out according to plan. The Celtics got there, all right, defeating Chicago, Atlanta, and Milwaukee while losing just a single game. For the Lakers, however, there was an unexpected roadblock.

The Houston Rockets were a 51–31 team during the regular season, winning the Midwest Division, but weren't considered a real threat to the Lakers. The Rockets gained momemtum, however, when they whipped Sacramento and Denver to reach the Western Conference finals. Houston was led by a pair of "twin towers": 7'0" Akeem Olajuwon and 7'4" Ralph Sampson. The Lakers felt their speed would more than compensate for the Houston strength underneath. But something went wrong.

Los Angeles won the first game, 119–107, with Kareem scoring thirty-one points. It looked like more of the same. But suddenly the Rockets got hot, especially Olajuwon. For some reason, the Lakers just played soft. Houston won the second game despite twenty-four points by Magic, then took the next three with Olajuwon scoring forty, thirty-five, and thirty points. In fact, they took the fifth game with Akeem the Dream in the locker room after being ejected, as Ralph Sampson became the hero with a last-second winning shot. The Lakers were eliminated in five games.

It was hard to explain what went wrong. It just seemed very difficult for any team to repeat as champs. Without the Lakers in the final round, Boston won again in six games, with the ubiquitous Bird becoming the playoff MVP once more. The Birdman was only the third player in NBA history to be named MVP during the regular season and again in the playoffs.

As for the Lakers, they had to regroup. The Rockets had exposed a definite weakness when L.A. couldn't throw a second big man out there to help Kareem. The problem wasn't solved until the following February when the club dealt for Mychal Thompson, a 6'10" veteran who could play both center and forward. Now Riley would have more flexibility up front, especially for the stretch run and the playoffs.

Several events also occurred in 1986–87 that would affect both the league and Magic Johnson. At age thirty-eight, Kareem finally began slowing down. He had to pace himself more, and, for the first time in his career, his scoring average would be below twenty (17.5). That meant someone had to take up the slack.

The other thing was the emergence of Chicago's Michael Jordan as the most exciting offensive player in the game. Jordan had been injured for much of 1985–86, but came back strong in the playoffs and now was set for a full season in which he would average more than thirty-seven points a game. Jordan's presence was still another huge boost for the NBA, which found the youngster nearly as good a league spokesman as Magic. He also emerged at the same time Larry Bird turned thirty. Once an NBA player moves over to the south side of thirty, his playing days might be numbered.

In fact, Magic (who was just twenty-seven) told an interviewer that December that the game was beginning to take its toll on his body.

"I was the youngest player in the league my rookie year," he said. "Now I'm the third oldest on my team. It seems hard for me to believe I've been here eight years."

Magic went on to say that he was feeling the bumps and bruises a great deal more. "The nicks and bumps take longer to heal now," he said. "I have to ice down my knees after every game. Three or four more years and that will be it. When you play eighty-two regular season games, then twenty or thirty more in the pre-season and playoffs, your mind and body can only give so much. I figure in three or four years I won't have anything left to give."

It could have been simply a low point. Many athletes talk about early retirement; very few actually do it. Those who love the game, as Magic Johnson obviously did, keep playing as long as they are physically able. It was hard to see Magic limiting himself, especially in view of the season he was putting together in 1986–87,

With Abdul-Jabbar's point production down, it was Magic Johnson who took up the slack. For the first time in his career, except for his abbreviated second season, he was averaging more than twenty points a game. Even with his increased scoring, he was also on a pace to top his career high in assists. So he had become a much more important part of the Laker offense than ever before.

The team had a 12–2 November; then, on December 12, they traveled to the Boston Garden and defeated the Celtics, 117–110, breaking Boston's 48-game win streak at home. In late December, when Kareem was out with an eye infection, Magic averaged 39.3 points and 13.3 assists over a three-game span, including a caeer-high of forty-six points in an overtime win at Sacramento. He was showing people a dimension of his game that hadn't been seen before. The guy who they said couldn't shoot was doing it all.

At season's end, the Lakers again looked like the best team in basketball. They finished with a 65–17 record, second best in club history, while winning a sixth Pacific Division title. And this time the brightest star in Lakertown was Magic Johnson. Playing in eighty games, Magic averaged 23.9 points and rolled up 977 assists. Better yet, he was finally recognized as the great all-around player he was by being named the NBA's Most Valuable Player, the first guard to win that honor since Oscar Robertson back in 1964.

Better yet, once the smoke of the preliminary playoff rounds cleared, the NBA got ready to put on another Laker–Celtic final. Boston was 59–23 in the regular season, but after sweeping Chicago in the first round of the playoffs, they had to struggle to a pair of seventh-game victories against both Milwaukee and Detroit.

The Lakers had an easier road. They swept Denver in three, defeated Golden State in five, then swept Seattle in four to get to the final round once again. They had to wait for the Celtics to clinch, then welcomed their greatest rivals to the Forum for game one. Each club had already won three titles since Magic and Larry Bird had come into the league. So this was a big one. The winner would have a leg up on the Team of the Eighties designation.

It was apparent from the beginning that the Laker game plan hadn't changed since the first time the two teams met in 1984. It was run, run, run. What made it more amazing was that they could do it successfully with a forty-year-old center. That was a tribute to three things—Abdul-Jabbar's condition, pacing, and savvy; Pat Riley's coaching, and the ability of Magic Johnson to set an offensive tone that kept Kareem in the game.

In the first two periods of the opening game the Lakers ran thirty-five fast breaks and only ten set plays in the half court. Not only did L.A. get the fast break off missed Celtic shots, but they were also getting breaks after Celtic baskets. That's how quickly they were getting the ball out and pushing it up the floor. A.C. Green, who was the new starter at power forward, took up where Kurt Rambis left off. He would get the ball after a hoop and put it back into play immediately.

When they had to set up their offense, the Lakers began going to James Worthy, who used his speed to blow past both McHale and Bird. Worthy ended up with a game high thirty-three points as the Lakers raced to a 126–113 victory.

In the second game, the Celtics tried to adjust. They assigned guard Danny Ainge to try to slow Magic down once he got the outlet pass as the rest of the Celts retreated down the floor. It seemed to work at first. After seven minutes of the first quarter Boston held a 21–18 lead and the Lakers had only gotten a pair of fast break hoops. Then the Lakers got a big lift from Michael Cooper.

Cooper, who would be the NBA's Defensive Player of the Year and was known more for the work he did guarding Larry Bird and the league's other big guns, suddenly became an offensive force. In the first half he hit four three-point shots, adding two more after intermission for a playoff record of six. He also dished out eight second-quarter assists. The Lakers won that one, 141–122, for a 2–0 lead.

The Celtics were in trouble. McHale was playing with a broken bone in his foot, and the other veterans just couldn't keep up with the Laker speed.

"If this continues," Larry Bird said, "maybe it's time to make some changes and get some people who will play hard every night and not just in front of their families."

Boston's sixth straight playoff road-loss was what

prompted the outburst. On the way back to Boston for the third game, someone asked Bird if the Lakers were capable of sweeping the Celts in four.

"Nah, we're just too good a team to be swept," he said.

Boston won the third game only because they suddenly got scorching hot from the outside. In the second quarter alone, the Celtics hit seventeen of twenty-one shots, most of them from the perimeter, to go up by four at 60–56. From there, Boston hung on to win it, 109–103. Bird wound up with thirty points, while Magic led the Lakers with thirty-two.

"Shooting over fifty percent is one thing," Magic said, afterward, "but shooting like they did is just beyond everything."

Until the fourth game, the players' passions seemed to stick to basketball. Some say it was because Magic and Larry Bird had finally become friends, doing promotions and endorsements together. Why shouldn't companies and the league use two of its most promotable commodities? It was a natural, and maybe it toned down the animosity between the two clubs. But finally, in game four, Worthy and Celtic reserve center Greg Kite got into it, and punches were thrown. Both benches emptied before order was quickly restored.

The game continued close and up for grabs. The Lakers kept trying to run, but the Celtics valiantly held them off. It was classic basketball, Magic and Bird driving their teams, prodding them, urging them to play harder. Both superstars were outspoken and vocal— before, during, and after games. They had been in the league eight years now and didn't feel at all inhibited about taking charge.

Finally, it came down to this: The Celtics had a 105–104 lead and Magic had the ball with just seconds left. This was one of those special situations, similar to those in '84 when he didn't deliver. As the clock ticked down, Magic drove across the key and threw up what he called "the junior, junior, junior skyhook." With two seconds left the ball dropped through the hoop. A desperation length-of-the-court heave by Bird was off the mark and L.A. had won it, 107–106, giving the Lakers a 3–1 lead in the series.

When asked how he felt about being down 3–1, Bird snapped. "How do you think I feel? I know that when I'm up 3–1, I say it's over."

With a chance to win it in game five, the Lakers faltered. Bird had railed at his teammates before the game, telling them, "If [the Lakers] want to celebrate, let's not let them do it on the parquet."

So the Celtics went out and played hard. The Lakers, with the exception of Magic, seemed to take the night off. Scott and Worthy shot poorly, as did Kareem, who hit on only eight of twenty-one shots in thirty-five minutes. Magic, however, wouldn't quit. He was everywhere, doing everything. One game story would describe his efforts this way: "For long stretches of the game, Magic appeared to be playing Boston all by his lonesome. Only he, it seemed, comprehended the fact that the Celtics were not going to quit."

Boston won the game, 123–108, to pull within one at 3–2, sending both teams back across the country for game six in L.A. Magic had scored twenty-nine points, grabbed eight rebounds, had twelve assists and four steals in the fifth game. He had played his heart out in a losing effort.

Then came the sixth game, and perhaps this was the game in which Magic finally achieved the total respect that would follow him for the remainder of his career. As usual, Boston didn't quit. They kept it close for the entire first half. The Lakers couldn't get the running game going, and whenever that happened, the Celtics knew they had a chance. Early in the third quarter each team was looking for a break, a chance to pull away. With 10:05 left in the period, Boston had a 56–55 lead.

That's when Worthy tipped away a pass from McHale to Dennis Johnson. He then pursued the ball, dove headlong for it, and tipped it ahead to Magic. Magic simply grabbed the ball and dunked, giving L.A. the lead by one. It also opened the floodgates.

Magic had only four points in the first half, but after the dunk, he just took over the game. Of the Lakers' thirty third-quarter points, Magic scored twelve himself and assisted on eight others. He also had four rebounds, was helping on the double team and in clogging the passing lanes. He was all over the place. During that period, the Celtics could manage just twelve points and the game was all but over.

"We just couldn't stop the avalanche," was the way Danny Ainge put it. Celtics assistant coach Jimmy Rodgers said that "the Lakers have a way of going through surges. That's what they're all about. It was more their doing than our undoing." When the game ended, the Lakers had a 106–93 victory and their fourth championship of the decade. It was a sweet one, maybe the sweetest. Magic had sixteen points, nineteen assists, and eight rebounds in the finale and was the unanimous choice as the MVP. He had duplicated Bird's feat of a year earlier, being both the regular season and playoff MVP. His performance and inspirational leadership were the talk of the basketball world.

"There's no question that this is the best team I've played on," said Magic, giving his teammates a lot of the credit. "It's fast, it can shoot and rebound, it has inside people, it has everything. I've never played on a team that had everything before."

Some said, in return, that a team never had a player who did everything the way Magic Johnson did. The subtle difference in 1986–87 was the fact that Kareem, at forty, had agreed to take a lesser role in the offense. That opened things up for Magic to really take over the team. Until then, he had always deferred to Kareem as the main man. As long as the basic philosophy allowed him to run, he was content to continue to work around Kareem. Why not? The big guy was basketball's greatest scorer. Magic was smart. He knew you don't cast aside a weapon like the sky hook. But he also knew that the sky hook was getting old and when it came time to do other things, Magic was ready.

Kareem didn't have to be told about the degree of Magic's contribution. He noted that his friend "played with enough intensity, at times, for the other four guys on the floor."

Pat Riley said what many basketball people knew, but the average fan might not have realized. The nickname "Magic" was deceiving. Earvin Johnson was not a basketball magician on the court. Even his spectacular passes had a definite purpose. As was pointed out, he threw fewer behind-the-back and between-the-legs passes than Bob Cousy had thrown in the 1950s and 1960s.

"It's partly the perception of the nickname that gives him the flashy reputation," said Riley. "I consider Earvin to be a player with fundamental flamboyance."

Since Magic and Larry Bird entered the NBA in 1979, either the Lakers or Celtics (or both) had been in the championship series every year. That should say something about the effect both players had on the NBA. Once again the Lakers had a goal, another motivation. Despite the dominance of the Lakers and Celtics in the 1980s, neither team had been able to win back-to-back titles. It hadn't been done since 1968–69. The Lakers would try again.

Magic's world was a very full one by this time. He

was so popular and well-known that he could travel in almost any circle, whether it be with people from the entertainment world who followed the team, corporate presidents whose products he endorsed, or his friends from the sports world. He was becoming one of the sports world's finest businessmen, and was already talking about owning his own pro basketball team some day. He had said years earlier that he always wanted to be in control of his financial destiny, and he kept his word. Though he never returned to Michigan State for his degree in communications, he made sure he understood all the ramifications of every endorsement deal, each investment, every request to spend his money.

He also increased his charitable work. His celebrity status enabled him to be an effective spokesman for a number of charities. One of his favorites was the United Negro College Fund and his work has netted millions for that worthwhile endeavor. Though he had dated Cookie Kelly since Michigan State days, the two still hadn't married, despite occasional rumors that they would. Otherwise, Magic's popularity was at its height, as was his reputation as a basketball player.

As he got set for the 1987–88 season, he was already being looked upon as something of an elder statesman on the Lakers and in the NBA. But he wasn't yet playing like one. He still felt like a kid when training camp began. And he still wanted to win on the court more than anything else in the world.

Magic

THE LAKERS WERE OUT OF THE GATE quickly in 1987–88, winning their first eight games. Kareem had decided to play another two years, including the present one, and was still the man in the middle even though he was nearly forty-one. But the team at this time really belonged to Magic. He was the leader and becoming more vocal. In his ninth year, he was a total student of the game. Basketball was his art and he had elevated the game to just such a plateau.

In that way, he and Larry Bird were totally alike. Both viewed the game as something more than running and jumping, shooting and defending. They both saw basketball as a composite picture, a whole that could be broken down into separate parts. They both knew just where those parts belonged and how to use them to the best advantage. They also both knew how to work with the hand they had been dealt, altering their own games to accommodate those playing alongside them.

The Celtics were an aging team, but Bird kept them winning. The Lakers, too, were now a veteran club and had Magic to keep them on top. Despite a succession of minor injuries that caused a number of players to shuttle in and out of the lineup, Los Angeles won another Pacific Divison title with a 62–20 record. The Celtics took the East at 57–25 and it looked as if the two clubs might meet yet again.

This time the road to the finals wasn't so easy. After topping San Antonio in three straight, the Lakers had to struggle for seven games with both the Utah Jazz and Dallas Mavericks before arriving at the finals. Boston didn't fare as well. The Celts whipped the Knicks in round one, then squeezed by Atlanta in seven before being upended by the Detroit Pistons in six games. So the Lakers would be trying to repeat against a new finalist, the rough, tough, up-and-coming Pistons.

Magic had missed some ten games during the regular season, but had what had become a typical year. He averaged 19.6 points and added 858 assists. He looked forward to a new challenge in the playoffs. The Pistons were led by guard Isiah Thomas, an all-star performer in his own right and one of Magic's best friends. The two would embrace before and after games. But when the ball was in play, it was war.

It was a playoff in which the Lakers had trouble with the Detroit defense. Forward Dennis Rodman was one of the best defenders in the league, and center Bill Laimbeer used every bit of guile to throw Kareem off his game. The Detroit defense held the Lakers under 100 points four times. Fortunately, L.A. won one of those games, the third one by a 99–86 count. Still the Pistons held a 3–2 edge going into game six.

Like most of the other games, this one was close all the way. Detroit had a 102–99 lead with a minute left, and it was beginning to look as if they would win the title. But Byron Scott hit a clutch jumper to bring the Lakers within one. After Thomas missed a jumper, Worth grabbed the rebound with twenty-seven seconds left. L.A. called a timeout, discussed the situation, then gave the ball to Magic as soon as play resumed. He dribbled to the top of the key, then started right down the middle but was cut off. He quickly got the ball over to Scott who went inside to Kareem. As the big guy turned to throw up a sky hook, Laimbeer bumped him and was called for the foul. Kareem calmly sunk both shots to give the Lakers a 103–102 lead with fourteen seconds left. The Pistons had a last chance, but couldn't convert and the Lakers had dodged a bullet.

Even with Isiah operating on a very gimpy ankle in game seven, the Pistons gave the Lakers all they could handle. This time it took an incredible effort by Worthy, who scored thirty-six points, had sixteen rebounds and ten assists, to enable the Lakers to win it, 108–105. It was a triple-double in the best tradition of his teammate, Magic Johnson. Worthy was the MVP and the Lakers had won their fifth championship of the decade. They had also finally repeated, winning two in a row.

A year later, Lady Luck would finally sabotage the Lakers. They went 57–25 in the regular season with the knowledge that it would be the final season for Kareem. The big guy had already announced his retirement at season's end and his great career was commemorated in every city the Lakers visited. It was quite an honor. It was also a year in which Larry Bird played only six games before having surgery on both his heels to remove bone spurs. So the times they were a-changing.

Not for Magic Johnson, however. With Kareem finally showing his nearly forty-three years, Magic again took charge of the Lakers and had a great year. He averaged 22.5 points a game, had a career high 988 assists, and pulled down 607 rebounds, his best board total since 1983. For his efforts, he was named the NBA's Most Valuable Player for the second time and was also named to the all-NBA first team for the seventh straight year.

In the playoffs, the Lakers caught fire. It was as if they all wanted to win it for Kareem. They reeled off eleven straight victories, becoming the first team ever to sweep three series on the way to the finals. Waiting for them once again were the Detroit Pistons. But just when it looked as if the Lakers would make it three straight, disaster struck.

Byron Scott was already sidelined with a hamstring tear and in the second game, Magic injured his left hamstring. There was just no way he could play. With both starting guards out, the Pistons won four straight to become champions and end the Lakers' reign. Two of the games were close, but without Magic, Los Angeles just couldn't get it going.

Over the next two seasons, Magic Johnson's stock as a basketball player and athlete continued to rise. When the 1989–90 season got underway, Magic was thirty years old. Just that fact alone must have made a lot of other people feel the passing of the years, especially those who grew up with him and had followed his career closely. Magic thirty? It sounded wrong, almost impossible. Wasn't it just yesterday he was hugging Greg Kelser after the pair led Michigan State to a national championship? And it seemed like just a year or two ago that he was playing that remarkable game to clinch the NBA championship for the Lakers. Oh yes, it was definitely hard to believe he was thirty.

Kareem was gone, of course, replaced by Vlade Divac, a 7'1" rookie from Yugoslavia. Many fans figured the Lakers would begin to fade, and so, perhaps, would Magic's zest for the game. But once again many underestimated the competitive fires that burned deep within Earvin Johnson. He saw Kareem's retirement as a challenge and he met it head on.

Somehow, Magic brought the Lakers through without missing a beat. He led them to a 63–19 season and another Pacific Division title. And he did it by putting together a simply remarkable season. Those close to courtside said he sometimes now talked his team through the offense, directing traffic like a cop on the beat. He would tell the young players when to cut, when to set a pick, what to do with the ball. It was a remarkable achievement in basketball generalship. But he knew the game so very well.

He also led the team in scoring with a 22.3 average, in assists with 907, in steals with 132 and was second in rebounding with 522. He may have been thirty, but he played like he was twenty. It was a virtuoso performance that would net him his third Most Valuable Player Award in four years.

The Lakers were an aging team and one that lacked an overpowering physical presence at center or power forward. They were fourteenth in rebounding and shot just forty-nine percent from the field, the first time since 1978–79 that they were below fifty percent. That made Magic's achievement in leading them to sixty-three victories all the more remarkable.

"As long as Magic is around, there will be the Lakers and then everyone else," said Phoenix coach Cotton Fitzsimmons.

Reserve guard Larry Drew, who joined the Lakers for the first time, marveled at the intangibles that Magic brought to the team.

"More than anything else this year I've noticed how he always finds a way to win," Drew said. "It's uncanny, but every time I thought we were out of it, he'd find a way to get us back in."

Pat Riley, who had watched Magic from the beginning, also saw the change in the first season without Kareem.

"Earvin came into training camp and just put the burden of the team on his shoulders," said Riley. "We just went on from there."

Magic admitted the new season presented new challenges.

"I had to do different things this year," he said. "My role changed and it was a challenge. Taking the three-point shot gave my game that much more versatility. It made me harder to guard. And without Kareem, I started posting up more than I ever had.

"By posting up and also looking for the three-point shot I'm not only running the show, setting the table for everyone, but I'm also actually involved as part of the offense. Suddenly, I had different responsibilities and it has been my most enjoyable time." Some of the other veteran Lakers like Byron Scott and A.C. Green didn't quite play up to expectations and that made Magic's performance even the more remarkable. Yet those weaknesses finally caught up with the team in the conference semifinals when the young Phoenix Suns eliminated them in five games. No miracles here. The only miracle, perhaps, is that Magic took the team so far.

The Lakers were expected to slip in 1990–91. For openers, longtime coach Pat Riley resigned. Maybe there were no more worlds to conquer, maybe he needed a rest. Riley would take a year off then emerge as the coach of the New York Knicks in 1991–92.

There were other changes as well. The team signed 6'10" forward Sam Perkins as a free agent. Perkins had been a teammate of James Worthy's at North Carolina and was a quality player. Michael Cooper was gone, veteran Terry Teagle taking his place. On paper, this was not as good a team as in the past. They would also have a rookie coach in Mike Dunleavy. So the Lakers were not a ballclub with great expectations.

Once again Magic was the driving force. On April 15, he broke Oscar Robertson's career assist record by getting his 9,898th in a game against Dallas. It was the record he was most proud of, because it bespoke of his unselfishness and his ability as a team player. He also continued his unique, on-court leadership, talking to the young players, directing traffic, and seeming to enjoy every minute of it.

The Lakers finished the season with a 58–24 record, second to the Portland Trailblazers by five games in the Pacific Division. There was no shame in finishing second. The Trailblazers were the new kids on the block, considered by many to be the best team in basketball. Magic averaged 21.8 points, second to Worthy's 22.4. Still, no one figured the team would go very far in the upcoming playoffs.

For openers, the Lakers were no longer a fast breaking team of rabbits. They relied more and more on a half-court offense. Some said it was because of the new personnel, others felt it was to preserve Magic's aging legs. If he didn't have to run as much, he could stay in the game longer. And this team definitely needed him on the court. When the Lakers upset the Houston Rockets in the first round of the playoffs, it looked as if the strategy was working.

It continued right to the Western Conference finals. That's when the Lakers shocked the basketball world by upsetting the Trailblazers in six games and making it to the finals once again. Some said it was a tribute not only to Magic's skills, but also to his tremendous will. He had simply imposed his will on his teammates and wouldn't let them lose.

Now the NBA had it going again. Waiting for the Lakers were the Chicago Bulls, led by the league's reigning superstar, Michael Jordan. The Michael vs. Magic matchup was viewed with the same great expectations that the Johnson–Bird matchups brought some years earlier.

Ironically, team roles were flip-flopped. It was Jordan and the Bulls who would try to run, Magic and the Lakers who would try to slow it down. Magic had tremendous respect for Jordan's scoring ability. As strictly a one-on-one player, Jordan might well have been the best ever. Now he had a solid supporting cast and the Bulls were heavy favorites.

"It's my job not to get caught up in this Michael vs. Magic hoopla," Earvin said. "I'm going to just try to do my job, which is to complement the other people, recognize what they are doing to us on defense and distribute the ball. If I get caught up in a scoring duel with him, I am going to lose."

After so many years of running and fast breaking, the Lakers now looked to pound the ball inside. Magic controlled the pace with the precision of a surgeon, running the twenty-four-second clock down as far as he could, keeping the pace slow and the Bulls from running. It was exactly the way the Celtics had tried to play the Lakers years earlier. Magic, being so versatile, could do it either way.

The strategy paid off in the opening game. Magic kept it mostly a half-court type game and Sam Perkins canned a three-pointer to put the Lakers ahead, 92–91, in the closing seconds. Jordan blew a couple of chances to win it for his team and the Lakers had the lead. Magic was right. He couldn't get in a scoring contest with Michael, who had thirty-six points and twelve assists. Magic had nineteen and eleven assists, but made the key pass to Perkins at the end.

But the Lakers' joy was short-lived. L.A. just didn't have the horses anymore and once the Bulls got it running, they really couldn't be stopped. They won the second game, 107–86, then the third in overtime, 104–96, and the fourth by a 97–82 count. The Lakers looked old, and tired, and outclassed.

"Michael is the scariest player in the league," Magic said. "He's been remarkable. He's raised his game, but he's getting a lot of help. Nothing we are doing is working. You just don't anticipate the series going like this. They are just dominating us."

One game later it was over. The Lakers had to play without James Worthy and Byron Scott, their places taken by untried rookies. Now there was nothing Magic could do to stave off the the final result. Jordan and the Bulls won the game, 108–101, to take their first championship. And to no one's surprise, Michael Jordan was the MVP of the finals.

The "changing of the guard" is inevitable in sports. The Lakers were undoubtedly the Team of the Eighties, winning five titles under the leadership of Magic Johnson and with Kareem Abdul-Jabbar in the middle. After the loss to the Bulls, Magic talked briefly about retiring, but as usual that didn't last long. After a short rest, the juices were flowing again and he began speaking about his goals for the future.

He wanted to add to his assist record, taking it over the 10,000 mark. In addition, he felt he could help develop some of the Lakers' talented young players while keeping the team a winner. And then there were the Olympics. With NBA stars eligible for the first time, Magic finally saw another goal within reach. He had missed the 1980 Games because of his decision to turn pro. It was no surprise when he was named to the team along with the other top stars of the NBA, including Larry Bird and Michael Jordan. That was going to be fun.

As always, he played summer ball and kept himself in good shape. In September, he married his longtime sweetheart, Cookie Kelly. Life seemed better than ever. Always an astute businessman, he even looked to the Olympics in Barcelona, Spain, as a way to spread his business interests to Europe, claiming there were "millions of dollars waiting for Michael [Jordan] and me."

Those who saw him play some exhibition games in France said he looked sharp, the same old Magic. No one knew then that his basketball time was short. Very short. No one, not even Magic, could possibly have known. But then came the fateful physical examination for a new life insurance policy, followed by the news that changed Magic's world forever. He missed the first three games of the 1991–92 season and right away people missed Magic. But, hey, he'd be back soon, doing his thing, making those beautiful passes, directing traffic, driving the lane, high-fiving his teammates, and smiling for the whole world to see.

Then came the press conference of November 7. It started at 3:00 P.M., Pacific Coast time. Within minutes, everyone knew. Magic broke the news that shocked a nation and brought to an end one of the greatest careers in the history of basketball.

BILL GUTMAN is a full-time writer and the author of more than 100 books, many of which involve the sports field. He has written histories, as well as biographies and profiles of the top performers in all the major sports, both past and present. His most recent books include a combination autobiography and recreation of the 1951 pennant race between the New York Giants and Brooklyn Dodgers, with former baseball star Bobby Thompson, as well as Young Adult biographies of superstars Bo Jackson and Michael Jordan. Mr. Gutman lives in Poughquag, New York, with his wife and two stepchildren.